Jim SHOMOS

Busybird Publishing
2/118 Para Road
Montmorency, Victoria
Australia 3094
www.busybird.com.au

A catalogue record for this book is available from the National Library of Australia

CONTENTS

Love Birds

"Underneath your tough exterior, you have a tough interior but deep down, you're hiding a beautiful heart. A real treasure. We might need a team of archaeologists, but when they uncover it, the love from your heart will radiate so much warmth and power, they'll put it in a museum because everyone on the planet will want to feel it, be touched by your heart."

PETER didn't breathe after his words tumbled out.

Jane was still. Too still. Leaning back on the balcony rail, not one thread of her honey hair moved.

Maybe I pushed it too far with the archaeologist gag.

His fingers interlocked, right thumb kneading left palm. He was tempted to head back into his loft studio and bring out the unfinished wine but it was almost breakfast time.

Jane shifted. Steamy dawn light created an angelic haze around her silhouette; too dark to read her eyes but not dull their blue flame.

He'd grown fond of their unlikely friendship, how their initial brief exchanges had evolved into night-swallowing chats. He didn't mean to upset her. He just wanted Jane to believe she could find love too. Could fall in love.

She deserves someone special in her life, someone to hold and -

Jane stepped close and kissed Peter on the lips, not like their usual hello-goodbye pecks on the cheek, a fiery kiss that launched a million messy questions.

Her hand slid under his ear and teased the back of his neck, triggering his arms to wrap around her waist; the sun rising between them.

Scorching. Crazy. Jaaane.

She gently pulled back, eyes brighter yet softer than he'd ever seen them.

"I love *you*, Peter. You're my damned archaeologist."

In a dark corner of his heart the tiniest voice whispered, *This is wrong… it's too soon.*

Christina only died five years ago.

Too late, screamed the rest of his heart and body.

As blood rushed back to his head, he accepted it wasn't only their heavy breathing in sync. He had fallen in love with Jane; Christina's closest friend.

When PETER spotted Jane parting the crowd through the market's lunchtime bustle, he straightened up and tightened his stomach. Jane's smile, framed by her glowing pageboy style, created a gliding beacon. He edged her height-wise, yet she'd cast a shadow across his path in the years since that balcony kiss, a shadow across his thoughts, a shadow across his heart. A private shade he cherished.

"Only you can make a black suit and white blouse look so elegant and spicy."

"Thank the Zimmermann girls," she said, waving off the compliment and stepped into his open arms. She kissed him then recoiled. "Ugh," she said, wiping sugar from her mouth with a tissue.

Spanish jam donuts were his traditional Vic Market guilty pleasure. He licked his lips, kissed a donut to paste more sugar on them then moved in again. She pulled two bananas from her bag and held them against her chest in a cross. He feigned fear.

"Eat whatever you want on your own, Peter, but I'd prefer to not watch you kill yourself." She passed him a tissue and he wiped his lips. "You're blessed with a metabolism that many middle-aged men would give up their TV remote for."

He enjoyed the way her eyes caressed his designer jeans and white shirt — which she happened to buy — and he did like the way they wrapped around his body, hinting at a more disciplined exercise regime than his weekly routine of zero.

"But you're forty now…"

Forty only feels old when someone else says it aloud.

He weaved his way towards a busker and placed the bag of donuts in their guitar case, along with a ten dollar note. Peter joined Jane on a wooden crate she'd claimed on the opposite side of the wide lane.

She offered him a banana. He ogled the donuts, contemplated diving back for the three remaining insulin grenades, then accepted her offering. Jane was right; however lucky he was with his body, at some stage he needed to start eating better.

"You look after me," he said.

Jane locked eyes with him, her head on that angle which always nudged him off balance. "You don't want to end up like the history of this place too soon," she said, waving her half-eaten banana in an arc. "This site was a cemetery years ago."

"Really?"

"One of my clients just told me, it was her school history project. We're stomping on the homes of nine hundred ghosts."

He stopped tapping his right foot to the rhythm of the busker's guitar. The tan R.M. Williams boots had survived Jane's unofficial makeover; he'd lost count of the amount of times they'd been re-soled. But it wasn't the market's buried history that sent a shiver through the leather, anything related to death always spun him back to Christina, to the morgue. He still couldn't develop a filter to stop that.

Jane had sucked in her lower lip, probably regretting steering their thoughts down that hole.

He squeezed her thigh. "Hey, I'll always love the Vic Market. It's kind of a microcosm of Melbourne." He took in the colorful stalls and characters hustling their produce, the tribes and suburban tourists. The busker changed tempo to one of Peter's favorites.

"Sweet groove," said Peter, admiring the teenager's courage for taking on George Harrison's *While My Guitar Gently Weeps*. He pointed his banana towards the busker. "I'm thinking about starting up again."

"Now? Are you finally having a mid-life crisis?"

"What do you mean finally?"

"You're in the classic range."

"I'm at the very early beginning of the range. Besides, we're not married, so I don't tick that classic box."

Jane's head tilted on that angle again, this time with a rare furrowed brow. It vibrated between his heart and ribs like an industrial fire alarm.

He focused on the busker. "I miss music and performing."

"You're kind of a performer now."

"It's not the same."

"Definitely pays better. You've invested all that money in your studio, yet haven't finished one song."

Hard to argue with the sandbags she dumped on his trickling creek of a comeback.

"Keep it as a hobby," she said. "Like my painting."

"Not the same. I need to bounce off people, like a band."

Jane pointed to a sign above a growing crowd further down the cobblestone lane: *LASTING SEX.*

"Speaking of performing…"

"Three wasn't enough last night?" he asked.

"I'm not complaining about… our core-strength work outs," she said, her tongue circled her lips. "But this looks interesting."

He recognized her sex diversion tactic, but Jane's eyes made him feel like a solitary cloud that had come across a stunning blue sky for the first time. He could float around them forever.

She bounced up and he followed as they shuffled to the back of the crowd. The full sign read: *LASTING SEX: LESSONS ON RELATIONSHIPS FROM AFRICAN LOVEBIRDS with Astral.*

He was skeptical about any lessons from birds and the obvious stage-name of the woman pushed his skept-o-meter into the red zone. Romance is organic and elusive and fragile; it doesn't need more complication by another artificial gimmick theory.

In flowing layers of black, orange and purple fabrics, plus matching hair, Astral stood beside a large aviary. Two lovebirds played affectionately in one section while one sat alone in the other.

"When lovebirds mate they stay together for life," Astral said. "If they don't have daily contact it can affect their health and lifespan."

He was about to dive in with a joke, but Jane's *don't even think about it* stare clamped his humor.

"The hen is on the left," Astral said, pointing to the pair. "See how affectionate these sweet lovebirds are."

The paired lovebirds gently stroked each other with their beaks, sometimes kissing or chirping as they explored their section of the aviary together.

"Now watch how this sweet couple resolve the issue of an intruding hen."

Astral slowly removed the board that separated the solo hen from the hen and cock.

For a few seconds nothing happened. Then the solo hen flew closer and perched near the couple.

The paired hen attacked. It was brutal and a few feathers scattered across the cage.

The crowd jumped back as one, forcing Peter and Jane to back away.

"Loving passion is a super-power but you can't be passive," said Astral as she separated the birds again.

The birds' reaction fascinated JANE.

She'd read about the lifetime mating habits of lovebirds but wasn't aware of their need for daily contact to survive. She wondered about similarities in human psychology and what could be learnt from these beautiful feathered creatures. Her mind flashed through images of famous couples like Linda and Paul McCartney, or Susan and Robert Downey Jnr, or — closer to home — her Aunt Cathy and Uncle John. Couples who almost never spent a night apart.

"You can't judge a book by its feathers," she said.

"Would you ever fight like that for me?" asked Peter.

"I wouldn't fit in the cage."

His champagne laugh didn't bubble inside her like it usually did. "Besides, those lovebirds committed for life. That's worth fighting for."

"Wow," he said. "Where did that come from?"

She stared at the lovebirds. She hadn't authorized those words to take off from her brain's runway; bit her lip in case other UFOs flew out of her mouth.

"You're the one who took forever to move in." Peter said.

"That was two years ago," she said, thankful Peter's direct attack snapped her back.

"A fun two years."

Jane made a so-so motion with her hand.

Peter stepped close. "I know underneath your tough exterior there's a tough interior, but deep under that—"

She put her finger over Peter's lips. Air traffic control in her brain had reconciled with her emotional radar and she'd worked out exactly what they were navigating. She turned Peter towards the lovebirds that had settled since Astral replaced the board. "Eventually we have to let her out of the cage."

Peter studied the three lovebirds.

Jane studied the metaphors and emotions she'd just dumped on Peter. What's the point of being a highly trained child-psychologist if she can't control the communication in her own relationship? This was supposed to be a quick catch up before her next client consultation, not a life-shifting discussion with Peter in a noisy, public setting that used to be a cemetery.

"I've got to go," Jane said.

"Already?"

She nodded and kissed Peter. She was about to head off but hesitated. "Sorry, Peter. Unlike most men, you've proven you can at least spell commitment."

"C..." Peter began, then contorted his face like he was struggling.

She slapped his arm and walked away. Peter caught up and stopped in front of her near the busker, who was munching on a donut. Peter's round russet eyes sparkled with mischief against his olive canvas; a Caravaggio meets Pixar. She couldn't paint him in a million sittings, yet he was framed in the gallery of her heart under warm lights. A solo exhibition. The only exhibition. She had to consciously restrain her hand from drifting under his wavy mocha locks, to not tease the back of his neck, their mutual "no way back" zone.

"C…" Peter teased. "C. A. G. E."

She heard the busker laugh, rolled her eyes and spun off.

"Come on, that was funny," Peter called after her.

Without turning around, Jane motioned so-so.

"See you tonight, my sweet little lovebird," he said.

It wasn't Peter's corny joke or lovebird line that lengthened her stride; it was her surprise at what she'd blurted out. True, she'd dragged her feet with Peter, even after their unforgettable first kiss on the balcony. Now she seemed five miles ahead. Some of those thoughts must have been swimming around in her subconscious and chose that moment to create a splash.

But really, Jane? "Committed for life"? That C-word is such a boring cliché.

Luckily Peter had turned it into a joke. That's what it deserved — ridicule. The "let her out of the cage" metaphor was OK. Christina would have been proud of that one.

Jane stopped on the path in the middle of Flagstaff Gardens and watched a fluffy white cloud float across the sky.

Let Her Fly

PETER had always marveled at Jane's clinical ability to get to the heart of an issue, especially when he hadn't recognized there was an issue.

"Eventually we have to let her out of the cage."

It wasn't until Jane held up that gentle mirror he realized how much he'd been clinging to the past, paddling through life with a subconscious anchor.

He needed more time to sort through exactly what it all meant for them going forward, but he knew a major shift had happened. A good shift, another balcony moment. He let the conversation with Jane kick around the back of his head as he ambled along the grass and around the trees in Carlton Gardens. Maybe he'd have a chat with his mom after work.

Work! He pulled out his phone and checked the time. Glen's going to be cranky. He cranked up his pace.

PETER placed his tablet on a table and faced the nineteen future leaders of the business and not-for-profit world. He could smell the ambition rising from these men and women, all in their late-twenties to mid-thirties. Making eye contact with each participant, they put away their gadgets and stopped doodling on their Glen Holmes Leadership Development pads.

Peter glanced at Glen, his balding senior partner, who was standing at the back of the room.

He nodded.

"Living your life without goals is like washing your car in the dark." Peter said, then clapped his hands. On cue, Glen switched the lights off, the room now completely dark.

"You might think you're doing a good job but you don't really know." Peter let the words drift around the room before clapping again. The lights flickered back on, with the future leaders on the edge of their seats.

"Today we focus on making decisions under pressure, and it all starts with your goals. Goals are your light." He picked up a marker pen and crossed to the whiteboard.

"If you are clear about where you're heading, you can make the most complex decisions in seven days." He wrote a big "7" on the board. "That's right, even multi-billion dollar decisions involving thousands of staff. Seven days." He circled the 7.

PETER leaned against the table, the war room empty. His boot tapped to the rhythm of the music coming from his tablet, lost in a YouTube video of his younger self, performing a pop-rock number at a pub with his band. Shot by a friend on a handycam, it wasn't a big room but they were rocking on a stage, so it must have been one of their later gigs. The camera zoomed in on a woman swaying with the music in front of the stage.

He paused on his favorite image of Christina. In her late twenties, with long wavy-brown hair — a poster-child for carefree fun — oblivious to the people squashed up around her, lost in the music. His music.

"I love that washing your car in the dark routine," Glen said as he entered the room, carrying two beers. Glen's energy and boyish smile suggested a much younger man than his fifty-five years, although without his shiny blue suit jacket he couldn't hide the hint of a little Buddha-tummy.

"So did I the first hundred times," Peter replied. He really had enjoyed performing on this corporate stage, as it was one way of using the psychology degree he had stumbled through.

He took one of the Mountain Goats as Glen plonked next to him. They clinked bottles and had a swig. The cold ale flushed out his corporate day and threw him even deeper into reminiscing at the pub with Christina.

"She was some girl," said Glen, looking over Peter's shoulder.

He smiled, nodded.

Glen clicked to the home screen that displayed a photo of Jane painting at an easel in Peter's garage. "But Jane's your future."

"And you're the expert on relationships?"

Glen had three children spread across two ex-wives. The first divorce was a brave step for him out of a poisonous relationship. The second divorce came when the love of his life found the love of her life, and it wasn't him. It would have broken many men but Glen had an endless supply of humor and infectious optimism.

"There's only one word for ending up old and single like me…"

Peter waited for the punch line, which Glen enjoyed dragging out.

"Viagra!"

He laughed and clinked Glen's bottle again, watching Glen continue laughing at his own gag. Strong friendships were like the deepest romantic loves; they had no logic in age or background. They just were. The older brother of one of Peter's ex-bandmates, the corporate-driven Glen had been the antithesis of Peter's dreams when they first met, but they clicked at a post-gig party and had been best mates ever since.

Glen pointed to the picture of Jane. "Jane's a seven-day decision, Pete. Huge decision and important…but indubitable."

Glen and Jane independently saying the same thing, in their own way, on the same day. Although Glen wasn't at Jane's award-winning Doctor of Psychology level of intelligence, he was more objective about this subject. He stared at the photo of Jane.

Seven days. Indubitable.

But there's one more person he needed to speak to.

"So, what do you reckon, Mom?" PETER asked whilst on his knees, watering three small pots on either side of the grave. "Do I have another marriage in me? Do I really deserve someone as special as Jane?"

"Don't waste your money on cut flowers when I'm gone. Get a small pot of everlasting daisies, the cute ones that look like mini sunsets. 'Sundaze Bronze' they call 'em. Have someone sprinkle a little water every now and then. Don't fret if they die, I won't haunt you for long," her final note had read. Gardening, mentoring and joking even after she died.

Peter admired the blooms. "Three years later and they're still going strong, Mom."

He put her old steel watering can down and sat on the ground, wrapping his arms tight around his knees.

"What if she gets bored and leaves me?" he said. "I couldn't live through that. Not after…" This was the first big decision he had to make without his mom's guidance, the "mother-meddling" he'd always complained about. Yet since her death, he'd missed her passionate spin on the world.

"You'd like Jane, Mom. She's beautiful and strong, just like you. And so smart it's scary." He wiped his brow with his sleeve. "I love her. I never thought I could love anyone again, but I do."

He eased into a comfortable position, picked up his guitar and strummed the delicate notes of his mom's favorite Beatles song, *Blackbird.* He sang softly, visualizing her on the back patio every Sunday evening through summer, when her eyes still twinkled, before her final days in hospital with breast cancer.

Entering the garage from the side door, PETER stopped when he saw Jane painting at her easel. A stream of afternoon sun cut through the high windows, creating a natural spotlight on one side of her face. He wished he could paint so that he could paint Jane exactly in that golden honey moment. She would never let him take photos.

"Take a picture in your memory," she'd always insist.

A glass of red wine shimmered on the corner bench amongst paints, brushes and cloths. Finished and unfinished paintings of birds, animals and landscapes leaned along a brick wall. He didn't recognize the classical music floating out of her phone, then again, he hated classical. *Pachelbel's Canon* was the only tune that didn't grate.

Jane put her brush down and picked up her wine. She'd lost her right arm below the elbow in her final year of primary school, a freak pushbike accident. Her fierce determination to not be a victim meant he didn't even notice the missing limb the first time Christina introduced him to Jane until they were saying goodbye. She'd taught herself to write and paint with her left hand, creating a series of visual stamps to prove life with one hand was no obstacle. He'd never felt sorry for her but was constantly in awe.

He glanced at the dusty tarp covering the old car on the other side of the garage. A super-quick glance.

Turning back to Jane, he caught himself straightening his spine and tightening his stomach. He chuckled silently at the silliness of his reflex action around her. Jane was good for his posture.

Quietly, he stepped back outside and wheeled in his surprise.

Jane looked up, her face scrunched with curiosity.

Pulling off the sheet, he unveiled a tall cage containing two lovebirds. He unbuttoned his shirt to reveal a t-shirt underneath with "I" above a heart-shaped outline with the word "C.A.G.E" inside. Her smile lit up the garage, which helped take the edge off his anxiety a little. He took her hand and knelt down on one knee.

"I love you, Jane Byrne."

Jane's drops-of-sky-eyes glowed. "I love you, Peter Christian." Her voice croaky.

He indicated towards the birds.

Jane searched the cage then caught her breath and squeezed his hands tight when her eyes found the burgundy velvet jewelry box at the bottom.

Bird poo plopped on the box.

They laughed.

He took the box out and wiped it with a towel, then opened the box to reveal a stunning diamond ring and matching platinum wedding bands.

His blood set new speed records racing around his body. He'd survived the hyper-vulnerability of proposing once before and never thought he'd be able to do it a second time. No matter how much he expected a "yes", the fear of potential rejection was impossible to bury. If it wasn't for Jane's unintended inspiration around the market lovebirds, he may have done it by email.

"Jane, will you marry me? Because bird poo is actually a good omen and—"

"Yes."

His eyes welled up as fast as his stomach unwound. He wanted to cling to this moment forever; to Jane's joyous face, to the warm syrup raging through his veins, to the super-sweet dam bubbling in his heart.

JANE didn't recognize the impostor inside her flushed skin, couldn't identify the jungle-drum beating in her heart. And who did this trembling arm belong to?

Her always reliable brain struggled, conflicted about how much Peter's proposal meant. It seemed like the word "yes" had been patiently hanging around, lurking in the shadows of her larynx, prodded by her heart.

Her phone sent out the melody of *Pachelbel's Canon*.

"As long as this isn't our bridal dance," said Peter.

Jane smiled, knowing his aversion to classical music but she was too entranced by the classic solitaire diamond to linger on one minor discrepancy in their relationship.

Peter steadied her hand then placed the engagement ring on her finger. The sunlight poured over her shoulder and sparkled off the diamond prism. How he'd remembered her fleeting comment about this ring, as they dawdled past the jewelers almost a year ago, she'll never know, but she loved him even more if that was possible. She kissed him and he tasted sweeter, if that was possible.

4.15am.

The red digits on the clock beamed through PETER'S eyelids. Despite his physical exhaustion from some of their best-ever lovemaking post-proposal, he couldn't sleep. It wasn't the solitary dog barking down the street, but an internal howling that had kept the lights on in his head.

He'd left Jane under the sheets, pulled on a t-shirt and boxers in the dark and ended up in the garage, sitting in the passenger seat of Christina's 1966 red convertible Mustang with the tarp and roof rolled back. He'd never worked out an emotionally viable way of dealing with her precious baby, so it just collected dust in his garage.

Emotions and memories flooded in from all angles, as if someone had ripped back a tarp covering his heart. He was sure he loved Jane and had done the right thing. One of the bonuses of getting engaged again was supposed to be a final farewell to Christina's ghost, but closure is the most elusive ghost; you can sometimes see it, never grasp it.

Why am I here? It's not helping.

He got out and pulled the tarp forward but his knees buckled. He leaned on the car with both hands and a single tear dropped onto the canvas, dribbled down the tarp and ran out of energy, worn down by the dust.

Hovering in the garage doorway, a cold shiver rippled across JANE'S spine. She wrapped her dressing gown tight, arms across her chest, sensing the painful memories Peter must have been working through. And fighting her own. In normal circumstances, there's no one she'd want to celebrate her engagement with more than Christina. Yet if Christina was still here, she'd never have connected this deeply with Peter.

A male colleague who specialized in relationships had warned Jane about the dangers of falling in love with a widower. The memory of a dead spouse was always molded in a perfect clay compared to the faulty material of any other ex-partner, but Jane had decided to take her chances and Peter had always been fully *with* her. Apart from this understandable milestone moment, Christina's spirit had never come between them.

In fact, Christina had pushed them together.

Like Peter, she was in a social void after Christina died; they both achingly missed her. Years later when she bumped into him at a psychology conference, their Christina stories burst out. They found comfort in catching up once a month to honor Christina. The monthly catch-ups became weekly, until that night on the balcony when she kissed him and accepted the depth of her feelings.

She stepped into the garage and wrapped her arms around Peter's waist, her cheek against his shoulder.

"She loved her old baby," Peter said.

"It would have made more sense if she died driving this rather than being run over by an SUV. She hated SUVs."

Peter turned to her. "Does any of this make sense? Chris was your best friend."

It was indeed a rare friendship. Christina and Jane had sat next to each other on the first morning of primary school and became soul sisters by lunchtime. They'd gorged on the fun, secrets and support of their friendship until her death.

"I miss her, Peter. There's not a day that I don't think about Christina." Jane wiped away tears with a tissue.

"For a while, I wished I had died with her." Peter barely whispered the words.

Another shiver rippled down Jane's spine. "And now?"

"And now… it's so weird how you and I reconnected. And fell in love."

Jane's relief flowed out with a breath she hadn't realized she was holding. She'd identified with Peter's mixed emotions early on. How could she fall in love with her best friend's husband, even if it was many years after Christina died? How much of their love for each other was real, how much were they simply projecting from their grief for Christina? She'd discussed it with a couple of other psychologists, re-read relevant chapters from her studies, even called her PhD mentor for the ultimate, most objective, academically definitive perspective.

She'd processed these clinical questions and feedback until it all became superfluous.

There was an unidentifiable period where their love transcended their history, transcended everything; as powerful in her heart as it was illogical to her brain.

"She would have wanted you to fall in love again," Jane said, "and the damned woman was always nagging me to let someone into my heart."

Peter nodded and half-smiled.

"If you're having second thoughts…" she said in a coarse whisper.

Peter wrapped his arms around her. His hug oozed endless safety, like her dad's hugs used to, with every other man hugs always seemed to have an agenda.

"No, no, definitely not," he said. "I love you, Jane. I trust you and I can't imagine being without you now."

"And I love and trust you, Peter." She kissed him gently. "I know Christina will always have a special place in your heart and that's OK."

Peter stared at her with deep love in his eyes, more Caravaggio than Pixar. He kissed her on both cheeks. She moved to the other side of the Mustang and together they finished covering Christina's car with the tarp. She ran her fingers through his hair then moved to the doorway.

Jane watched Peter study the simple shrine to Christina he'd made seven years ago on the wall beside her Mustang. It had a giant poster of her hero, Ayrton Senna, with an entourage of favorite singers and bands. Some crushes Jane had shared, like Bowie, but others like Doc Neeson from The Angels were all Christina's.

Peter joined her at the door and turned off the light.

Honeymoon Haze

"Yikes!" squealed JANE.

Peter had nearly dropped her as they bumped through the hotel suite doors. "I'm sure it was easier last year. Have you put on weight?"

Jane thumped his chest. "Maybe you're getting old?"

"Maybe the dress is more slippery this year."

Jane had scoffed at his idea to wear their wedding gear for their first anniversary celebration, but was glad Peter had insisted. Other restaurant guests congratulated and joked with them. It added a sense of magic and fun.

"Agh!" She clung tight as he spun around and headed to the bedroom. He barely made it in time, half-dropping her onto the king-sized bed.

Peter stood back, eyes wide, cheeks glowing, tie loose. He'd never looked sexier. He'd even ditched his old R.M. Williams for the black Batsanis boots she'd bought him for the wedding.

"They're not real men's boots if they've got zips," he'd complained in the store. But he looked spicy in them and he'd packed them voluntarily for this anniversary celebration.

Her hair had been styled up and a couple of locks had strayed down her face. She blew on them from the side of her mouth. Her strapless gown had slipped down a little, the white satin blending in with the silky white bedcover.

"Wow," he said. "It's like you're floating on a cloud."

Becoming one white-hot cloud.

"Not your words I need right now, Jon." She patted the bed.

"Ah, my beloved Ygritte," he said, in his hopeless impersonation of her *Game of Thrones* hero, Jon Snow. The show was her one guilty pleasure during studies and ridiculous hours in the early work days.

He let his jacket slip off his shoulders to the floor, then threw his tie. She caught it, grinned, and threw it over her shoulder. He unzipped each boot slowly, his smoky russet eyes never leaving hers.

She unzipped her dress and leaned towards him, revealing more of her cleavage. "I hope you brought your battle sword," she purred.

She'd had other lovers to scream home about, but Peter was so in tune with her body. Thank Goddess Athena that her two-month involuntary libido sabbatical was over; work had often swamped her, but it had never drowned her desire for Peter until the last couple of months. He was right, they needed this anniversary honeymoon to reactivate their…core strength workouts.

Peter moved to the bed, in his best warrior-swagger. He took off his belt and swung it like a sword over his head; it flicked back and hurt his hand.

"Ow!" he said, dropping it.

She laughed and pulled him on top of her. Her inner-Ygritte yearned for more than humor…

On the balcony PETER sipped orange juice and gave a nod to the architects of the Azabu suites. They'd made the most of the tropical forest views while creating a private sensual oasis. Byron Bay had turned on a humid morning, so he hadn't bothered with a top. He rubbed his hip through his boxers.

"Tender?" asked Jane, relaxing on a cushioned chair in a singlet and panties, hands clasped over her stomach, her long legs stretched and crossed at the ankles. It was a miracle they both didn't end up with more bruises, the way her body drove him into a sexual frenzy.

"I'd fall off any bed with you anywhere, anytime." He took a bite of a raspberry and peach muffin. A teapot and cups were laid out on the table with a fruit platter, a whole pineapple serving as a centerpiece.

"This is a lovely present, Peter. I'm glad you forced me away from work." Jane kissed the back of his hand.

It had taken some effort to organize the seven-day break. Jane's relentless work and research schedule was taking its toll on him and her assistant, Maria. Jane blamed it on the stress of the keynote speech she was preparing for the International Child-Psychology Conference in Singapore. When he and Maria presented their plan for this little post-conference break, Jane had lashed out. "How can I trust either of you when you sneak around like spies behind my back?"

It took three days of walks, massages and lazing around Byron Bay for Normal Jane to surface. Thankfully, just before their actual anniversary dinner, she was back in form and he was ready. Like an adult virgin ready.

He picked up the pineapple. "This reminds me of you."

Jane threw him a glare.

"On the outside it looks uninviting and even dangerous, yet on the inside it's sweet and juicy with wonderful texture."

Jane kissed him. Must've been the salt in the humid air because usually his schmaltziness bored her.

She picked up a mango. "And this is you. Sensitive skin, sweet and mushy inside, but with a core strength that's all heart." She placed the mango next to the pineapple on the table.

"I'm glad I had our wedding gear sent up here in advance as a surprise," he said. "That was fun last night."

Jane nodded. "Very sneaky."

He winked as he chewed his muffin.

"And sweet," she added. "Very sweet. I have a couple of surprises for you too." Jane handed him an envelope.

He opened it and glowed at the Qantas airline tickets. "Italy?"

Jane nodded. "And Southern France and Spain. Three weeks. No work. Just you and me."

"Wow, three weeks. Wait till Maria finds out."

Jane smiled. "She'll probably take the credit."

"Hey, we can go to Arenal Sound!"

Jane shot him a questioning look.

"The music festival near Valencia," he said. Arenal wasn't

as famous as other international festivals but the spectacular pics and clips he'd seen of punters raging to music on the coastline stamped it on his musical bucket list.

"I don't think we'll have time, Pete. We'll see."

"That's OK, Arenal isn't a biggie."

"I was hoping for three weeks of slow villages, hidden private art galleries, and meandering through local bazaars."

"It will be amazing whatever we do."

Three weeks away was a huge step for Jane. "So, you said two surprises." He waved the tickets. "I don't think you can top this."

Jane picked up a strawberry and placed it between the pineapple and mango.

He stared at the fruit. Something slushed around his gut and it wasn't a smoothie. "We're going to open a fruit shop?"

"A family business."

Peter had never seen Jane look so vulnerable. "I'm… I'm late." She rubbed her stomach.

The silence between them clanged like a village church bell. The first thought that crawled in was the responsibility, an absolute point of no return. Marriage was one thing but becoming a dad threw his whole life into another dimension that demanded instant maturity.

He bit some muffin and chewed on all sorts of tangents. Jane's news explained why she hadn't been drinking alcohol lately. It probably explained some of her other stuff too; the unusual bursts of anger and the severe headaches weren't from the pressure of her keynote presentation on top of her self-imposed workload. Stress multiplied by hormonal mayhem.

"Are you OK with this?" Jane patted her stomach.

"Yeah… yeah, of course. It's just a big…"

"Shock?"

"Surprise."

It's not as if Jane had bought a car and he could say he didn't like the color but he's happy for her because she's happy. In coupledom, this was as major as it got. Not the time to stumble into dumb responses.

"Are you sure you're OK? We never planned this."

"I love you Jane, and I love being with you. Anything that happens around our love is only going to be good." He rose and held out his hands for a hug.

Jane's eyes filled with tears and her chest sagged as she let out a huge sigh. She stood and hugged him tight. He gently wiped tears from her face with the back of his finger. Jane kissed him then turned to face the forest, snuggling back into him. He placed his hands over her stomach, barely touching her singlet.

Among the million thoughts hammering around his head, this was the final nail in his musical coffin, *Goodbye Yellow Brick Road* to those dreams. He'd never forget the painful tone of his mom's mantra, inspired by his dad.

"Following dreams is selfish. It ends up hurting people who care about you."

After Christina's death he'd dutifully finished his degree and fallen into Glen's partnership offer. But just below the surface of his work, he'd always clung to the idea of getting back into music. Giving one more crack at becoming a pro performer, maybe writer-producer. But this wasn't a mere sign for him to finally let go, it was a solid wall directing a permanent detour.

Jane buckled slightly and he propped her up. "I still make you weak at the knees?"

"Ha! Just the sun going to my head. Ready to unwrap your last present?" Jane said as she turned to him. This time he was grateful for the sex-diversion, no matter how temporary.

Jane came in for a kiss, but suddenly her eyes rolled up and her bottom lip quivered. Her body went limp.

Peter caught her before she fell to the ground.

Double Blur

JANE didn't complain about Peter squeezing her hand so tight. She'd grown to love his tactile nature. He hated hospitals; the one place fear and pessimism conquered his optimism. Following the scary blur of the previous twenty-four hours, who could blame him?

She'd recovered quickly at the hotel, although still a little hazy. Peter had insisted on an immediate return to Melbourne and they went straight from the airport to the hospital. After blood tests, MRIs and X-rays, she just wanted the all-clear to go home.

She had no doubt the overnight stay was overkill until she saw Dr Starkey's face followed by an even sterner woman's face. It's never a good sign when two doctors walk in together. Her body found a strength missing since she'd fainted; defensive tension setting up barriers, setting her back straight, setting off alarm bells in her brain.

"This is Dr Zeng, our head neuro-oncologist," said Dr Starkey.

Neuro-oncologist…

Her hand tightened around Peter's.

"I'm afraid the news isn't good. Jane, you aren't pregnant."

As gentle as Dr Starkey's tone was, his words speared her womb.

Breathe, Jane, breathe.

Her clinical brain dived into auto-diagnosis. The presence of a neuro-oncologist made it hard to fight facts; some of her physical issues over the last couple of months flashed by.

Breathe, breathe.

She didn't want that news… it couldn't be…

"Jane, you have three brain tumors. And the tumors are all quite advanced," said Doctor Zeng.

"It's a credit to your strength that you've survived this long," said Dr Starkey.

Jane's eyes searched Peter's, pleading for a crumb of hope they would wake from this nightmare. For the first time ever there was no light in his eyes, no spark or flicker anywhere on his face.

Her hand gripped his so tightly, his skin was red and her knuckles white, but she couldn't feel anything. Even her brain hit a wall; a cold gray wall.

On the studio balcony above his garage, PETER raised his acoustic guitar high and threw it down hard. The guitar crashed onto the concrete driveway with a final distressed twang from the strings which ended up like umbilical cords between the detached neck and body.

Beside him, Glen winced. Peter ignored him and picked up an electric guitar from the adjoining stand just inside the French doors. He smashed it against the timber balcony railing, and again, then a third time. The neck bent and a few strings snapped. He hurled it. The body broke open on the concrete, spilling electrical guts, the neck on a right angle. The two mangled guitars lay a few feet apart.

Glen's hands on his shoulders helped him turn away from the wreckage and Glen led him inside. They slumped onto the couch, facing the dusty mixing desk and two large blank computer screens. No wisdom bounced back from the studio tech gear.

Silence screamed at him.

"First Christina, now Jane. Am I a jinx?"

"Don't be silly, Pete. None of this is your fault. It's no one's fault."

"How can this happen twice?"

Glen shrugged.

"Jane's parents say it's God's way. How stupid is that?"

"Ludicrous," Glen agreed.

"What kind of God would take two women like that? What kind of God would put me through this?"

"Pete, I can't begin to imagine the pain you are going through. But right now, it can't be about you. You have to be there for Jane." Glen wrapped an arm around his shoulders. "You have to be strong for her."

Peter nodded. "I have to be strong for her." He stared at the two empty guitar stands. "I don't know if I can." His hands interlocked on his lap, right thumb rubbing hard on his left palm. "I don't want her to die." The last syllable launched heavy, violent tears. Glen tightened his grip around Peter's trembling shoulders.

"You're the best man I know, Pete. Whatever it takes, you'll be there for her — minute by minute, hour by hour, day by day."

Peter's heart howled with pain because he knew his precious time with Jane would fade out in reverse; Jane would disappear day by day, hour by hour, minute by minute, breath by breath.

JANE sensed Peter behind her, even before he placed a fresh cup of chai on the bench. He kissed her neck and she took in a slow breath as his lips lingered on her skin, reacting mostly from muscle memory. The drugs drowning her body killed much of her physical sensation, along with the pain. Peter had bought a comfy stool with a leather back and sides to help her stay at the easel longer, a new necessity as her body weakened at the same time as her need to paint increased. One of the painful paradoxes of dying.

Peter rested his cheek next to hers and wrapped his hands gently around her dwindling body. She didn't have time for too many paintings but was determined to finish this one. She'd never felt like an artist, just a hobby scratcher but wanted to make it decent. Her goodbye gift for Peter.

Six months maximum, probably three. That was the scenario painted by her doctors, based on the size and position of her tumors. "Inoperable," Dr Zeng had added. Soon she'd be bedridden in intensive care.

She put her brush down, wrapped her arm over Peter's, closed her eyes and inhaled him as deep as her lungs would let her. He must have showered with the natural lemongrass soap today, the one they bought from the Vic Market a few weeks ago. Cinnamon from the chai wafted across, as well.

"It's beautiful," said Peter.

Opening her eyes, she only saw the flaws. "I've gone overboard with the streak of sunlight."

"No, it gives it a kind of spiritual tinge."

"The lovebirds are OK, I'll give you that."

"It's all beautiful. I love it." He kissed her bandana.

"I'm about to add…" Tears betrayed the strength she was trying to show; a regular pitfall the last few months. She snuggled into Peter's bicep.

"I know," he said. "I love this painting. I love you."

She reminisced about the velvet ring box and Peter's ridiculously romantic and creative lovebirds-proposal. His tears converged with hers, gravity and sadness trickling them down her cheek faster than her heart pumped blood through her body. The thought of not having a future together was unbearable, so they found themselves reliving moments. Some reminiscing they did together, some in silence, both desperately floating around fragments of memories that made up the mosaic of their relationship.

JANE soaked in a bubble bath, her eyes closed. Apart from hopeless sadness, two emotions had seeped through the most since the diagnosis; her guilt at putting Peter through this kind of pain for the second time in his life, and the urgency to feel alive by spoiling all her senses while she could still feel anything.

Why didn't I take a bath more often? I should have painted more. Why didn't I take more holidays with Peter? Why didn't I recognize the signs earlier? If I did, maybe they could have stopped it, or at least slowed the tumor.

Arvo Pärt's fluffy musical cloud *Spiegel im Spiegel* drifted around the many candles and her favorite vanilla-scented balls, bought on their anniversary trip to the Byron Farmers Market. Her eyes tightened when she recognized the cruel irony.

Her brain had always been her proudest asset, given her so much satisfaction and reward, but now it rotted with a sickness that took away everything.

She opened her eyes and couldn't help chuckling. Peter stood in the doorway beaming, holding a basket of long-stemmed red roses in front of his navel, but otherwise stark naked.

"You make me laugh, even at the saddest time of my life." Her voice barely reached him.

He winked at her, kissed a rose and threw it into the bath. She picked it up and blew the bubbles off towards Peter. He kissed another rose and threw it into the bath as he shuffled forward, then another…

PETER kissed a rose then threw it onto Jane's coffin.

He'd let Jane's Catholic parents dominate the funeral arrangements, as he was in no state to organize anything, but he insisted on this final moment alone with Jane.

Weighed down by all the support people had dumped on him in kindness, he didn't have the strength to carry his own thoughts anymore, let alone other people's useless words. He wiped his hand on the pants of his dark wedding suit. He knew she'd have wanted him to wear it with this silk tie and those fancy zip-up boots.

He kissed the final rose slow and gentle, then dropped it onto Jane's coffin.

"Death is hard on the living," said Glen, slumped on the back seat of the limousine next to PETER.

"Death is hard on the living," Maria repeated like a prayer, making the sign of the cross, sitting opposite him.

Death is hard on the living. The only clear, cold logic Peter had heard recently. Staring through the window towards the grave he wondered what on Earth normal is now. He looked up for answers but all the blue sky offered were a couple of fluffy white clouds drifting together. He may as well have been on them.

Jane might be in a grave but the planet wasn't big enough to bury his pain.

New Arrival

PETER had heard some ridiculous ideas from Glen before and this one topped them all.

"Mate, it's been three months," said Glen.

Three months. He'd struggled with any sense of time since Jane's funeral.

"No. No way. A holiday is the last thing I feel like having right now."

He leaned against the balcony doorframe and scratched his beard. It still felt weird; he'd never grown one before.

Glen wrapped an arm around him and looked around the room. "Mate, that's exactly why you need a holiday."

Peter followed his eyes. He once would've been embarrassed by the sad movie cliché — littered with pizza boxes and other takeout food containers — but embarrassment was an emotion he didn't have energy for. The studio had become his cave. Staying in the house was too difficult, too many memories tapping on his shoulder. The studio couch had a scrunched up blanket and a pillow at one end where he'd been trying to sleep during the last three months.

"I'm not going to let you rot here for the rest of your life," said Glen.

"I've earned the right to rot here if I want to."

"Jane would want you to go."

Glen was right. If there was an afterlife, he wouldn't be surprised if Jane was orchestrating this whole thing. But that's ridiculous; there is no afterlife.

"I can't do that trip on my own. It was an anniversary present."

"I'll come with you."

"I know you're trying to help, Glen. I appreciate everything you've done, I really do. Especially sneaking my dirty clothes away to wash them. But I'm not going anywhere."

"Pete, you can't bring Christina and Jane back. We get to live, so we owe it to them to make it count."

We get to live, so we owe it to them to make it count. It's probably what both women would have told him in their own way.

"When?" Peter asked, surprised the word had squeezed out.

"Tomorrow."

"Tomorrow! That's crazy."

"You might not be a barrel of laughs but you need this."

"I couldn't even be bothered packing."

"Maria's already packed your bag."

Maria had become awfully good at secretly colluding on other people's holidays.

Peter clutched one more straw. "I can't leave the birds."

The lovebirds in the aviary downstairs were all that had

kept him sane the last few months. If it wasn't for their needs, he probably wouldn't have left the studio at all. They were the only witnesses to his engagement with Jane. He'd fed them, cleaned the cage, stared at them and mumbled to them, and he slept under Jane's painting of them. Her final painting.

"Maria's promised to look after the parrots," said Glen.

"They're not parrots they're—"

"Lovebirds," Maria shouted as she bounced up the stairs into the studio. "I promise I'll take good care of them. I Googled everything about them last night and you know me, if I say they'll be looked after they will."

Maria pinched her nose, marched straight to the balcony doors and opened them wide. "Phew! It's amazing you and the birds can survive this stench."

She pushed Glen aside, grabbed Peter's shoulders and locked eyes. "Glen is right. Jane would be devastated if you didn't go."

"I've booked tickets for that Spanish music festival too," said Glen over her shoulder. "Arenal Sound!"

The lovebirds' chirping filtered up the stairs; they seemed to be encouraging him too.

He looked towards the stairs, at Glen with his silly smile then back at Maria. He didn't have the will to argue anymore, he nodded.

"Fantastic," Glen slapped Peter on the shoulder.

"But first, you need a shower," said Maria as she started cleaning up.

"And a shave."

Glen guided him to the stairs. "We'll see some great soccer and the Spanish women, *alegria*!"

A pizza box bounced off Glen's back.

"Ow!" squealed Glen.

Peter turned to see Maria miming a Frisbee throw with a devilish grin. Skin started cracking on his face as he smiled for the first time in months.

"OK, no women," Glen said. "But real churros, yes! Spanish donuts in Valencia!"

Glen was so excited on their journey that PETER had to reward him with some level of energy. It must have worked because the last few hours were the longest period he hadn't thought about Jane; probably because the mass of bodies and blaring music was somewhere she would never be with him.

He'd shuffled out of a tiny corner cafe across the road from the Valencia beach, juggling two bottles of water and a bag of churros. A thirty-three degree afternoon, he would have preferred to cool down with a *helado* but Glen was eager for Peter to have "real churros, mate".

His t-shirt was soaked from the heat in the packed café and he was grateful for the slight breeze. He looked up and down the busy street for Glen. The aroma of the churros plus the bustling crowd took Peter back to his quick lunch catch-ups with Jane at the Vic Market. That's all it took; a smell, a sound and he was instantly overcome with pining.

How do you create any distance from someone who is fused into every part of your being? He ached for Jane to turn up and throw his bag of churros in the bin. He'd give up sweets, give up anything if he could have her back.

A familiar loud whistle made him turn like a tired old sheep dog. Peter spotted Glen waving both arms high on the beach side of the road.

Peter stepped between two parked cars and instinctively, for an Australian, looked right down the road. He stepped out and as he turned to check the other direction, a speeding car bounced him into the air.

PETER spun in the air amongst the churros and bottles of water yet felt no pain. The spinning stopped but he continued floating.

The car screeched to a halt thirty yards down the road. Two young women closest to the horror screamed, which triggered a chain reaction of hysteria. People started circling his body on the road.

His body.

On the road.

Glen burst through the crowd and dropped to his knees, a tiny figure as Peter continued floating away yet his slumped body broadcast Glen's pain for miles.

Death is hard on the living.

Silence. Sweet, embracing silence.

PETER continued rising, now in a large clear tube, swallowed into the sharpest, most striking blue sky. Safe, warm, at peace.

A montage of happy images featuring people and events in his life flashed past on clouds outside the tube. The early visions are familiar, despite being from before he was old enough to remember. He saw rare moments with his dad, many with his mom, Glen, Christina, gigs with his band, Jane, Glen and Maria in his studio…

The smells and emotions of those times filtered through with the images as he slowly drifted up the tube. Magical, surreal.

A buzz of joy flowed through him as he began heading down, like when he was a kid hurtling down the giant slide at the local pool. The images of his past were replaced by a kaleidoscope of colors. The silence only magnified their beauty.

PETER rolled out of his tube onto a thick soft mattress. He lay there for a while, a little dazed.

He slowly sat up and ran his hand along the deep blue mattress fabric. His fingers and palm could feel the velvety texture, so his sensory touch seemed OK. There weren't any signs or posters to give any clues as to where he was; some kind of booth with three timber walls, about nine feet high and a plush curtain across the front that closed in the middle. There was a solid timber desk in the other corner and two wooden chairs.

A small wooden plaque engraved with "9" hung over the front rail. There wasn't a ceiling on his booth; his eyes enjoyed the vast maze of intertwining tubes like giant grape vines.

Between the tubes he glimpsed a glass roof and beyond, stunning blue.

His ears adjusted to the murmurs and sounds coming from beyond his booth. He couldn't make out anything specific, just the background hum of many people in a large enclosed space. For a moment he wondered if he was in a Spanish hospital. But there wasn't any hint of medical equipment or that medical smell, nor the usual tension hospitals provoked.

Plus, he felt OK. No pain or blood. No scratches or bruises on his arms. The legs below his shorts were unscathed too. He stomped his sneakers. No pain. Strange, because he did remember being hit by a car.

He closed his eyes and rested his face in his hands, elbows supported by his thighs.

Maybe I thought I was hit by the car and it missed me.

He focused hard to recall his last movements. The cafe and churros… walking out onto the street… Glen's whistle… crossing the street…

"Woo-hoo!" A nearby shout of childlike joy from a woman.

Peter got up, climbed onto the desk and peered over the wall.

"Welcome, Dawn! I'm Bec," said a bubbly woman holding a tablet.

Dawn looked to be in her late-seventies and fit in leisure-wear and sneakers. "That's the best fun I've had in years." said Dawn, pointing at the tube and mattress.

Bec unleashed a deep laugh, almost dropping the tablet.

Dawn leaned close to Bec with a mischievous glint in her eye. "Are there any naughty men here?"

"Yes, and we allow naughty women too."

Dawn shrieked with laughter and threw her arm around Bec. "I think we're kindred spirits."

Peter shook his head. This was no hospital, unless it was a mental institution. But why would he be thrown into…

This is crazy!

He peered into the suite beside his.

"If there's no football, I wanna go to the other place. And what's the beer like?" asked a guy in his early-twenties wearing an Arsenal soccer shirt, to a middle-aged man in Victorian-era clothes, including top hat.

Maybe he was dreaming about some unique theatre troupe rehearsing different scenes? The subconscious could play weird games.

He looked around for more clues and was stunned by the scope and design of the building. The tangled mass of giant tubes separated as they reached the bottom and disappeared into spaces like his. Behind a massive floor-to-ceiling glass wall were glorious trees with vivid green, red and yellow leaves, and flowers of every color. Jane would love to paint this.

In those unusual early moments, wherever he was, his eyes seemed to feel rather than merely see. Not a gravity force, nor weightless, a visceral inner peace.

"Sorry I'm late."

Peter spun out of his spiritual moment and lost balance. He had to jump off the desk and onto the mattress. He steadied himself before facing the guy who was reading off a tablet.

A round face supported messy silver hair. It wasn't long; it just didn't seem to have attracted the attention of a comb. This dude didn't have any fashion sense either, despite the contemporary clothes but his smile, in most circumstances, would have made him an instant friend.

This wasn't most circumstances.

"You scared me to death," Peter said.

"Um… I'm a bit late for that too."

Is this idiot the hospital clown for adults? A counsellor with a lousy sense of humor?

"Where are we, what is this place and who are you?"

"I'm Keith," he said, throwing out his arm to shake hands. Peter cautiously lifted his hand and Keith shook it with an enthusiastic vigor Peter couldn't return.

"Congratulations, you've made it Up Here."

Peter whipped back his hand. *Up Here?* He wasn't sure what that meant but his extreme inner-peace bounced to the other end of the spectrum.

Keith waved the tablet. "I was waiting in Arrival Suite 6. Silly me. You were in 9. Got those two mixed up since primary school."

"Up here? You mean I'm in…?"

"Yes. Exciting, isn't it?"

"Like Hell, it is!"

Keith winced and looked around nervously.

Peter heard Dawn's piercing voice. "Did someone say Hell?"

The Arsenal dude yelled. "Hell?"

All around the building hysteria broke out; some people sobbing, some shouting, "Hell, we're in Hell!" Some prayed, others chanted mantras.

A calming male voice boomed across the huge space. "Ladies and gentlemen, boys and girls, please calm down. You are not in Hell. I repeat, you are not in Hell. You are in the local Arrival Lounge for Heaven and I am your Arrival Manager."

The sound was so good for such a vast space, Peter instinctively searched for speakers but couldn't see any. Everyone calmed down. Some thanked various gods.

"Welcome, all of you. Please return to your Arrival Angel and they will help you with anything you need to know."

Peter examined Keith. If this *is* Heaven, they sure got it wrong on Earth with how angels look.

"You're my Arrival Angel?"

"I prefer to think of myself as a transition consultant," Keith said.

He studied Keith. "Transition consultant…?"

"Yes, yes. I'm here to help you through your early days. Like a tour guide."

"I'm in a coma. You're my doctor and I'm hallucinating." Keith shook his head.

"This is crazy. For starters, I'm an atheist."

Keith clicked through the tablet. "Yes, yes, I see. Lucky your first name is Peter. And your surname is Christian. That's a bit ironic, isn't it? Knock-knock. Who's there? Peter. Peter who? Peter Christian. Come in."

Something about Peter's face ended Keith's chuckle.

"Sorry," he said. "I think that joke died before you did. Let's get you home."

"Home?" Peter looked up at the high roof and colorful, winding tubes then back at Keith.

Keith placed his hand on Peter's shoulder, sending a relaxing warmth through him. Keith's blue eyes oozed so much kindness that somewhere deep inside, a small part of

Peter began to accept this could actually be happening. He might be in Heaven and Keith could be real… whatever real meant Up Here.

"Yes. Your home. You're going to have to trust me a little. Try not to analyze everything. Process each moment as we go through it. Give your soul time to adjust."

Keith headed out of the suite.

Give my soul time to adjust?

Keith popped his head back through the curtains. "Come on, before they change their mind."

Peter stared at the gap in the fluttering curtain.

Before they change their mind? To what? Is that another joke?

He dragged himself up. His senses were more alive than they'd ever been, yet at the same time, he was dazed and confused. He'd had lots of time and reasons to contemplate death and the afterlife; too much for someone his age.

Right then, in the majestic building with its weird glass tubes, fluffy mattresses and arrival-angel-transition-consultants, his brain was out of its depth.

He shuffled after Keith.

Parallel Universe

PETER studied what looked like normal people go about their business the same as on Earth. He knew the road they were on well but it wasn't quite the same.

"Physically, it's a replica," said Keith, crunching the gears on his vintage Holden Kingswood.

The eight lanes on the tree-lined St Kilda Boulevard catered for a variety of transport: vintage and modern cars, bicycles, horses, buggies and trams. They cruised by a lot of travel agents, cafés, hobby and leisure stores, counsellors and therapists on one side, trees and gentle green hills of the park on the other.

"Replica?"

"Yes, like a parallel universe."

"But how do you fit everyone?"

"The number of souls has only really become an issue in the last hundred years. Plus we manage things better.

It's amazing what you can achieve when there is no crime, pollution, or wars."

He struggled with the basic notion that he'd died, let alone ended up in a utopia Heaven.

Their car chugged past the Shrine of Remembrance and gardens on their right. Keith seemed to be taking a longer route to his house, but Peter was too distracted to care. This must be a dream. A wild, vivid dream that his mind was using to cope with Jane's death, or his own injuries.

"This is a dream. I'll wake up in my hotel in Valencia and Glen will—"

Keith shook his head with a sympathetic glance.

A billboard caught Peter's eye: *HOUDINI TRAVEL ADVENTURES – WE GET YOU THERE, YOU FIND YOUR OWN WAY OUT.*

If this was a dream, it was one of his most creative. If you're in a dream, all you have to do is start falling and you wake up. Dreaming or dead, he had nothing to lose.

He opened his door and jumped out of the moving car.

"Peter!" shouted Keith.

Peter rolled out of control into the bicycle lane and knocked over a cyclist. The tar road was solid but no pain hit him. Still no bruises or abrasions on his bare arms and legs. Weird.

Keith stopped the car and jogged back to him. Cars swerved to avoid them. A small group watched them across the lanes from the park.

"I'm still here," Peter said.

Keith nodded.

The cyclist, aged in his seventies, maybe eighties, dusted himself off and checked his bike, which hadn't been damaged but there was a rip in the guy's bike shorts.

"I didn't feel a thing," Peter said.

Keith helped him up. "That's right, we don't feel pain."

"I'm on morphine. That's why I didn't wake up."

"Another cynic," said the cyclist. "I don't know why they let 'em in."

"Takes all kinds," said Keith.

"Ever since church attendance numbers started falling, the standards of entry have been deteriorating." The cyclist glared at Peter.

"Well, I'm sorry for ruining your little country club, but I've had bit of a lousy day," said Peter.

The cyclist swung back onto his bike. "And they got no manners," he said and then pedaled off with the energy of a teenager.

The edgy little exchange seemed all too real and certainly didn't feel heavenly. In fact, he was fired up much more than something like that would usually affect him.

"If this is supposed to be Heaven, where's the compassion?" he asked, pointing at the cyclist.

"The cyclist cruising happily till you knocked him over?"

Peter's inner-fire chilled instantly; the abrupt change in extremes stunned him and he placed a hand on his chest and stomach. It wasn't painful but it wasn't normal.

"Is this some kind of sign? Am I not supposed to be here?"

"Takes all kinds," said Keith.

Keith pulled up outside PETER'S house.

Peter got out and stared. It was exactly like his house, including the loft music studio he'd built on top of the garage. And most of his neighborhood had looked the same on the way through.

Keith joined him in the driveway.

"This is totally weird. Is… is Jane…?"

The thought that Jane might be inside overpowered his atheism and skepticism, and whatever other "ism" he was going through. He walked, then jogged, then sprinted to the front door and dived inside.

Peter rushed around the house, calling her name.

No Jane.

In fact, there was no sign of her living there at all; he didn't find any of her clothes, her makeup, not even her vanilla balls in the bathroom. Only Jane's bigger touches, like the red gum dining table, red leather couch, the bold stripes rising from halfway up the walls.

Keith watched him, sitting at the table. Peter couldn't sit; he hovered nearby.

"I don't get it," he said. "If we're really here, why isn't Jane here?"

"Jane chose to live in an apartment nearby."

"That doesn't make sense. Why?"

"You'll have to ask her."

"She knows I'm here?"

Keith nodded.

That didn't make sense. Surely if he was in Heaven and Jane knew, she'd be here. He checked the albums and CDs on the shelves. Everything as he knew it, filed in eras rather than artists and genres.

"Maybe Jane didn't move into the house before I died because she didn't want to be here without me. I would have felt the same way if the timing was reversed."

"Maybe."

He picked up a vase and dropped it on purpose and jumped back as it smashed to pieces on the floor.

"Things can break?"

"Yes, but not us. We don't feel physical pain."

"Sorry. I'll clean it up later. If I'm still here." He never did like that vase anyway.

"It's your vase and house. No need to apologize to me."

"So, where is she now?"

"At work."

"Work? Why would anyone work in Heaven?"

"Because it's a wonderful environment to work in. No bullies, lots of support. Souls still have curiosity and untapped talents. Dreams they never achieved. So they work, they study and there's plenty of time for fun."

It sounded like Keith was trying to convince him there was a Santa Claus. Peter stood on a chair and spread his arms.

"What else can I do in this fairytale? Fly like Peter Pan?"

"Only in one direction." Keith pointed at the floor.

Peter stepped off the chair. "So what's your deal? Were you a trained counselor or social worker?"

"I was a priest. Now I prefer this work."

"Catholic priest?"

Keith nodded.

"This is all so… so weird. Do you hear that a lot?"

Keith nodded. "All the basic information you need is in here." He pointed at the tablet on the table. "It has the contact details of everyone you know Up Here."

Peter bounced to the phone on the side table. "So, I can just call Jane and say, 'Hi, honey, I'm home'?"

"Yes, you can call Jane. And Christina."

That stilled him. "Christina…" The name slipped out as a velvet sigh. For the first time in nine years, her name wasn't wrapped with the horror of her death. The caressing contrast was palpable.

Christina. He sat at the table and stared at the tablet, sensed Keith staring at him. Against all his beliefs and instincts, some part of his soul craved for Keith to be real, craved for it all to be real. He could really hug Jane. Talk to Christina.

A tangible, physical, powerful warmth gushed through him, swirling inside whatever his body was now.

"You've had two great loves, Peter," Keith said. "But you only have one eternal soulmate."

The warmth whooshed out. It took him a moment to adjust to the sudden change.

"One soulmate. Now we're back to the fairytale."

"Only if it has a happy ending."

Not for the first time in the last couple of hours, he was confused.

"We're talking about eternity here," Keith said. "A real 'forever after'. Forever is a long time to be with the wrong person. Some couples get irritated with each other after a few years over little things, like the way they say certain words, or the way they pick at their food."

"Or leave the tap dripping," Peter said.

"Imagine if you're stuck with that person forever. In eternity," said Keith.

"That would be Hell."

"It's fascinating how often that word comes up in Heaven, even from atheists."

Peter slowly spun the tablet around on the table with both hands, half a circle at a time.

"Get it right and you have eternal bliss," said Keith.

"I've never had to choose between Jane and Christina," he said to the tablet, to himself.

"It's not so much a choice, more like a discovery. Plus, this isn't just about you."

"How long do I have?"

"Well, I'm assigned to you for seven days but—"

"Of course, seven days. The ultimate irony… seven days."

"Peter, you don't have to decide right now. There's no time limit on-."

"It's OK, Keith. I get it. Most people do everything they can to avoid big decisions. But making tough decisions is one of my things, it's what I preach." He emphasized "preach" with his fingers.

He clicked the tablet on. Photos of Jane and Christina split the home screen. Seeing them together as equals for the first time emphasized his new reality. He'd never had to think about Jane and Christina as wives in the same time dimension before. They were part of his linear life; one only happened after the other was gone. Something brewed inside him again, more physical than emotional; an energy that ushered cynicism and all its negative buddies out the back door.

"Can I have some time alone?" He partly asked the question to test the boundaries, to see if he actually had any control or choices.

"Of course. You're in Heaven, not prison." Keith headed to the front door.

The doorbell chimed.

Peter jumped up, bundling his chair over.

Keith stopped in his tracks and stared at him.

A visitor was the last thing Peter expected and the familiar chime acted like a wake-up bell, telling him to get with the program.

Keith headed the other way. "I'll sneak out the back. If this is Jane, you should be on your own the first time."

Peter wrestled a barrage of thoughts and feelings. Jane. At the door. Crazy!

Peter put his chair back at the table then tenderly walked to the front door, afraid to create any sound on the polished floorboards in case the whole experience disappeared. Now he was desperate to believe.

He stopped for a moment to try and settle the warmth flaring inside him.

Jane…

He tip-toed quickly back to the tablet and looked at the photos of Christina and Jane next to each other. He clicked on Jane's photo so it filled the screen.

Every ounce of logic and confusion melted by euphoric yearning.

He could hold Jane again. In his arms.

He rushed to the door and swung it open.

"Oh," he mumbled, disappointed.

"Oh? Is that how I brought you up? Oh?"

Linda Christian scrutinized him in her all too familiar, born in the 1950s way.

Vitality shone off her like in his boyhood memories, yet in the older image of herself pre-cancer.

"Hey, Mom."

Her super-moon smile launched his and they hugged; a timeless loving hug that felt real by any definition.

She stood back to observe him. "You're looking a little pale and confused."

He nodded. "Confused doesn't really cut it."

"Come on, tiger. Let's get you a big lunch."

This whole scene could easily have been brought on by his comatose subconscious because food had always been his mom's solution to anything. When he surfaced from his bedroom in his early-twenties at two in the afternoon, fragile from his hangover, it was, "Let's get you a big greasy breakfast". When his last girlfriend before Christina dumped him for another band's lead singer, she said, "Let's get you a big dinner". She cooked with love and ate with passion. Many a tear had fallen on her plate, but mostly tears of laughter.

Mom wrapped her hands around his arm and guided him out the door.

"Yes, this is a parallel universe, but some aspects have evolved differently Up Here. There's more of a community focus. A village feel. You'll love it," said Linda.

Sitting on a grass embankment, PETER took in the friendly atmosphere amongst approximately one hundred other... people? Souls? They were spread across the grass and on seats in front of the small stage of the amphitheater, a new addition to the Yarra Bend Park he knew. Nestled around the snaky Yarra River and surrounded by a variety of trees, dominated by towering gums, you would never have guessed that downtown Melbourne was just a few minutes' drive away.

"These are delicious," he said, as he took another bite of his meat boreka.

"Everything's organic," said Linda. "Plus, because we don't feel any physical pain, all sensations are heightened, including taste. Delicious jumps to a new dimension."

Keith mentioned the heightened sensation principle earlier, but he wasn't exactly receptive then. On reflection, he couldn't ignore how he'd actually experienced the heightened sensations thing: the angry fire with the cyclist, the sweet warmth when he thought of Jane at his door. As his mom and taste buds reinforced the concept, his resistance started to dilute a little more.

"You always believed in this," he said, sweeping his arm around.

Linda nudged him with her elbow. "All those Hail Marys paid off."

"But why am I here? All I ever did was make fun of the church. Did I get in because of you?"

Linda seemed to take forever chewing, then sipped her juice. "Peter, don't try and work everything out straight away. It can become overwhelming. One thing you have plenty of Up Here is time."

She seemed more settled; maybe she'd lost some of her anger. She hadn't aged at all, looking better than before she was diagnosed with breast cancer. And she wore more color; an orange silk scarf splashed across her deep green blouse.

With light blue jeans, she sent out an energy matched by the sparkle always bubbling in her green eyes.

"You look terrific, Mom. Have you… you know… done some work on your—?"

Linda's laughter made him smile. He'd missed the sound of her infectious cackle.

"You haven't read your information kit have you?" she asked.

"Haven't had time."

"You can stop your physical aging process whenever you want to. But spiritually and mentally, you continue to grow."

He thought about this as he surveyed the variety in the crowd. Some women were in Victorian-era dresses and gloves, with their partners in top hats and tails. Others clad in more recent fashions and there was a scattering of ancient Greek or Italian robes.

"Physically you stop… but spiritually and mentally you grow," he repeated.

Linda nodded and picked up another boreka.

"Like vampires," he said.

"What is it with vampires? All the young folk want to know about these days is sex and vampires."

"Or sex with vampires." Jane had a theory about this: as religion was ignored more with each decade, younger generations seemed to be obsessed with characters and stories connected with the afterlife, especially vampires and zombies.

"You must have a million real questions. Ask me anything."

"Have you seen God?"

Linda smiled and shook her head.

"Are you happy?"

Linda watched an affectionate couple lying near them and when she turned back her eyes had lost a little sparkle. He knew why.

"Yes," she said.

"Surely my father isn't around here."

Linda picked up her bottle and took a big swig of her cranberry juice. When she put it down, she shook her head.

"Serves him right the way he walked off on you. He's probably in—"

"Ladies and gentleman."

Peter was interrupted by the booming voice of the announcer from the stage PA system.

"Please welcome our special guests today, all the way from the USA… Abbott and Costello!"

Two actors walked onto the stage and began the "Who's On First?" routine.

He looked at Linda and she nodded, smiling. A moment of weird déjà vu; they'd watched the old buddy movies together a million times in his teens. He smiled as Costello got confused about the names of players in Abbott's baseball team. This was his all-time favorite comedy routine.

Peter leaned close to Linda. "They're really good. From here they look like the real guys."

"They are the real guys," said Linda.

He put down his boreka and leaned forward studying the stage. He'd become a little suspicious again that it must've been coming from his subconscious, but the performance mesmerized him.

Linda nudged him. "Have you seen Christina yet?"

He crashed out of his comedy comfort zone and glared at her.

Mom sticking her nose in my business. Nothing's changed except the location.

"Mom, don't interfere."

"I'm not interfering. It's a simple question."

He wasn't sure if he was annoyed with his mom, or just wanting to delay the whole question of Christina and Jane.

"Christina is your destiny," said Linda, eyes on the stage.

"You don't really know Jane. You've got to give her a chance."

"If Christina didn't die you would never have fallen for Jane."

"Maybe Christina died so I could fall in love with Jane."

The Mexican stand-off was another déjà vu moment that was all too real, as was his mom's look. Uncannily similar to Jane's; the same angle and hint of eyebrows closing over her eyes, with the same intensity.

"Thrown us onto a little carousel argument, haven't I?" she said.

He nodded.

Linda picked up a boreka. "You're right. I shouldn't interfere. Try the cheese, it's amazing."

He accepted her peace offering and bit into the creamy feta pastry. The flavor and texture was amazing but while he watched the show, he couldn't help relating his growing confusion and frustration with Costello's, like family dynamics and circular arguments about destiny and fate.

The one thing his mom had managed to do was throw a powerful spotlight on the only issue he couldn't ignore. The two major parallel universes in his life, Christina and Jane, had now merged into one very weird space as his ex-wives. He had no idea how he was going to align those stars.

Which one does he contact first?

Riding the Elephant

When PETER saw Jane through the hallway window his stomach instinctively tightened and he straightened his back.

He almost burst into laughter at the idea he was actually looking at Jane. Spending time with his mom went a long way to making the bizarre Heaven experience real. Seeing Jane and recognizing his familiar physical reaction was compounded by the warmth gushing through him again; it was so powerful that he had to prop himself up with a hand on the wall.

He'd phoned the school to make sure it was OK to surprise her during work hours. He loved hearing Jane's new title of Chief Connector. According to the school's website, it wasn't about teaching or preaching to the kids; it was all about connecting with them. And Jane was the best connector with kids he knew. It was her gift. Especially troubled children and teenagers.

He straightened and checked out the class. Jane sat at the rear while a Facilitator — that's what they call teachers — worked with nine children between the ages of eight and ten. All of the children were having fun and were involved with the Facilitator except one girl who sat on the floor away from the others. A curtain of black curly hair hid her face as she rhythmically pushed a metal toy bus into a wooden chair leg.

Jane was focused on her, then looked up at him. He could see her mouthing his name, as if she couldn't believe her eyes.

He poked his tongue at Jane and her smile launched towards him like fireworks. She hurried into the hallway and he hugged her with all the power he had. Summer after winter. Sweet melody after punk. Spanish donuts after Brussels sprouts.

"Janey's got a soulmate, Janey's got a soulmate," the children sang out from the classroom.

He pulled faces at them. Jane blushed, took Peter by the arm and guided him away.

It wasn't till they'd been walking in the school gardens for a while when PETER noticed Jane's full right arm and right hand. He stopped and pointed at it.

Jane nodded. "Strange, isn't it? When I rolled out of the tube, it was just there. I keep forgetting about it, knocking stuff all over the place."

He ran his fingers over her "new" hand and arm. Jane closed her eyes and took in a deep, slow breath.

"It's real… not a…"

Jane opened her eyes and smiled. "Very real."

Floating in her eyes was the realest thing since he rolled out of the tube.

"Come on, I'll show you my favorite spot," she said.

Harpo House was not like any school Peter had ever walked through. It fitted the zaniness of its founder, Harpo Marx of the comedy brothers' fame; the one with the wild curly hair who never spoke, but captivated audiences with his visual antics and musical prowess.

There were bright buildings like a giant Lego village, the only double story complex featured a series of winding slides as exits. Kids didn't need a second invitation to whiz down them. The playgrounds included vast grass areas, mazes, flying foxes, quiet reading nooks and creative play spaces with some equipment and designs he'd never seen.

Three ducks followed them along the pond. Jane stopped under the willow trees; a peaceful little hideaway.

"Thank you for those last few months. You were really special," said Jane

He raised Jane's hands and kissed each one gently.

"I know it was tough on you," she said.

"Not as tough as the time you made me sit through a whole opera."

"I don't know how you put up with me; I was so grumpy and ugly."

"I knew I was the only beneficiary in your will."

"A lot of good that did you."

He laughed and laughed and laughed. Bent over, leaning on his thighs laughter on the outside, euphoria flowing inside.

"Let's be clear, to me you were never ugly and no one could blame you for being grumpy. You were in ridiculous pain and dying. Grumpy was an amazing achievement, I would've been a monster."

Jane gently ran her fingers through Peter's hair. He closed his eyes, immersed in the electricity of her caress. He gave up all notions of being in a coma or hallucinating. If this wasn't real, let it be a dream that never ended; but for a moment he was terrified this might only be a dream so he flung his eyelids open. She was still there, her blue eyes softer than he remembered them.

"It's really you," he said as he stroked her face.

Jane leaned close and he met her lips. The unmistakable melding of her sensitive mouth with his created a fire beyond any of their kisses on Earth. When he eventually withdrew, the burning was ravaging way past his lips. He didn't let go of her.

The softness in her eyes had been replaced with a hunger. She wasn't in a hurry to let go either.

"Wow," was all he could muster.

Jane nodded as her gaze strayed between his eyes and lips. She grabbed his arm again and guided him back to the school. "I'll show you my office."

"A private soundproof office?"

She slapped him with her new hand and knocked him out with her old killer smile.

Heaven.

JANE struggled to believe Peter was sitting next to her on the office couch. She'd never wished him death, even after discovering Heaven, and now her heart and lungs and tummy burned with joy.

She had to divert some of his attention, dilute her inner-fire, so she showed him a video introduction of Harpo House. Peter focused on the big screen on the wall that dominated her office. She'd missed those eyes, his boyish excitement at the simplest things. She was also surprised by the power in their kiss. She'd had more time to adjust to the notion of heightened sensations Up Here, yet she could never have imagined the sweet-chili sensations sizzling through her.

Focus, Jane. One step at a time.

When the role to head Harpo House was offered to her she had snapped up the opportunity without blinking. The resources and energy devoted to children was beyond her wildest dreams. She knew children died but it was still a shock to see so many Up Here. To contribute to their adjustment and mental wellbeing was a privilege, never work. Once a connection was made, the healing process for children moved quickly. They had an innate power to be in the moment. Making that connection after children had been wrenched from their parents, their siblings, their life; that was the clinical challenge.

On the screen, a Facilitator worked with nine children.

"No class has more than nine students," said Jane. "This is Roman history. Now, guess what this class is." She flicked the remote to show a different classroom.

A Facilitator and students wore Ancient Roman costumes, all engaged in a play. The 3D visual background made it look like they were in Ancient Rome.

"Drama?" said Peter.

"No, same subject. Ancient Roman history."

"History was never that much fun when I was at school."

"Exactly. We adapt the teaching methods to suit the children. Some are more right-brained, yet most of the education systems on Earth focus on left-brain methods. Some are shyer and need more attention. Some kids need constant attention. We don't have to force round pegs into bureaucratic budgets."

Peter's russet eyes were wider and more penetrating than she remembered.

"What?" she asked.

"I always loved your passion."

"It's not just Harpo House. Every school Up Here is creative and lateral. Because there's no crime, war, or pollution, the resources for kids are amazing."

"You're amazing. Being with you again is amazing… amazing."

Peter put his palm tenderly on her cheek. She ached to close her eyes and absorb him. All of him.

"It will be good to have you home again," he said.

She snapped out of her dreaminess. It took all her will power, especially since that pond kiss. There was one obvious minefield she wished they could avoid but they couldn't. She was determined to do the right thing. For all of three of them.

She had to be strong.

Peter moved in for another kiss but she eased back and placed his hands on his lap.

"Peter, I love you. You know that. And I can't tell you how good it is to… I missed you so much."

"I missed you too. I—"

"But I can't move in with you."

Peter's face scrunched up. "If this is real, why can't we just take up where we left off?"

"Because 'we' now includes Christina."

Peter slumped back on the couch.

"You have to see her Peter."

His eyes confirmed he knew she was right. Christina was his wife and her closest friend. Now they were all together.

"How is Chris?" he asked.

"She's… good. Really settled Up Here."

It wasn't a lie; Christina was settled. Jane didn't share the delicate point that she and Christina had only caught up once in the three months Jane had been Up Here. It had been a short catch up, with just five words spoken between them.

From the moment JANE realized where she was, the one person she wanted to see the most, and the least, was Christina. Despite their deep friendship, or actually because of it, she didn't know how to be the messenger on the one bit of news Christina would be most interested in: Peter.

The torturous dilemma unbalanced her more than discovering she seemed to be in some sort of heaven. She stalked Christina from a distance twice. First where she worked, at her go-kart track called Sennasation. Jane was so proud of how Christina had created this little haven for her passion with cars and speed, but she couldn't take the extra fifty steps to tell her.

On her second night Up Here she sat near Christina's Richmond warehouse apartment. Building up courage and carefully structuring the words in her head, she had watched the parallel universe spinning around her. There was a different feel to Bridge Rd; not the shopping end which was Christina's type of nightmare, but further east where funky cafes melded with quaint stores from the 1800s.

Jane started towards Christina's apartment then froze. Whatever else she was unsure of in the previous couple of days, she was definitely not ready to face Christina. So, she had turned around and headed in the opposite direction.

And there was Christina, bouncing towards her like the concrete pavement was her personal trampoline.

When Christina caught Jane's eyes, she froze. Jane was swept up with joyous warmth which overpowered her contentious mission. Christina's smile competed with the neon lights of the Bridge Rd strip and passing vehicles. She closed the gap in one bound, almost jumping into her, wrapping up twenty-eight years of friendship in four excited arms.

Jane released her grip. Christina was smiling through tears, but must have sensed something in Jane's eyes. Christina stepped back with narrowed eyes. She could never hide anything under Christina's laser glare.

After all the careful compilation of words and practiced tone, three words flew out like a spear.

"I married Peter."

Christina clutched her chest where Jane's verbal spear had landed and her joyous warmth turned icy. Thick, Arctic ice. The three words reverberated between them, echoing louder and louder.

"My Peter?" Christina's incredulous tone was barely audible yet ferocious.

Part of her admired the way Christina's two-word question pursued her logical need for clarification, while her heart expressed rage.

Guilt paralyzed Jane. Despite all her training, intelligence, clinical experience and all the bond built between them, she didn't know how to take that incendiary conversation beyond those five words. She watched Christina hobble away like a wounded deer, seeking refuge in the darkness of her lane.

Jane wondered if their whole history was now buried in those shadows.

*

"Jane?"

"Yes, Christina and I caught up after I arrived and we're catching up again soon." White lie. Healthy white lie.

"That's good," said Peter.

JANE had planned to see Christina again before surprising Peter, but didn't regret Peter out-surprising her. She would get in touch with Christina again. She couldn't control Christina's reaction, but if she was the first to bring out the peace pipe and made sure Peter faced up to Christina, she could move forward with Peter with clear consciences.

"You haven't agreed yet," she said to him.

"OK, I'll see Christina."

It was definitely the right path, yet she couldn't loosen an unfamiliar knot in her stomach.

"If you agree to catch up with Mom," added Peter.

The knot slipped up to her neck and tightened. She hadn't thought about Linda at all; it was hard enough getting her head around facing Christina. It wasn't that she and Peter had done anything wrong, it was just the complexity of the situation.

Linda always made her feel like she'd done something wrong and Jane never understood it.

"Oh, dear. An eternal mother-in-law," she said.

"You can talk to her about vampires and sex."

"Yeah, right. Or zombie relationships."

From the beginning, Linda and Jane may as well have been zombies. Linda was always polite, but she just obviously didn't like Jane. Christina sensed it, Jane knew it. Linda died before Peter and Jane started dating, so she hadn't had to face her. Now she couldn't avoid it.

"You two will get on like Thelma and Louise."

She stared at the blank screen. "Yes, we know how that ended.

Noisy and brutal.

Standing next to Keith as he coached a wheelchair rugby team, PETER was surprised by the fiery aggression. Male and female players rammed each other's wheelchairs trying to get the ball or stop an opponent progressing with the ball over the touch line.

The community sports stadium featured a roof made mostly of timber and glass, similar to the walls on three sides. The other side was taken up by terraced wooden seating with about fifty fans who were very involved with the action. The cacophony of wheels spinning on the polished timber surface, cheering spectators, players and coaches yelling, and the violent clash of metal wheelchairs was not what he expected when Keith suggested they meet there.

"Smash him, Joe! Smash him!" yelled Keith.

Joe crashed into the side of a man's wheelchair, which made the guy spill the ball.

"Good hit, Joe. I'd pay to watch that," said Keith.

He tried to reconcile the placid Keith he met the other day with this Doctor Jekyll. "Were you really a Catholic priest?"

"Thirty-five long years."

"Why did you leave the church?"

"One day I realized…" Keith glanced at a couple of men laughing and cuddling in the stands. "I hadn't laughed in years."

One of Keith's players made a breakthrough and looked like getting the ball to the end line.

"Go, Angie, go," he shouted. "All the way, Angie!"

As she neared the touch line Angie tried to pass the ball to a teammate but missed him and the ball ran out.

"Damn!" said Keith.

"I see your sense of humor is really flowing now."

Keith ignored him. "Angie, when you're near the end line you must be like the devil."

Angie gave Keith a thumbs-up. The opposition coach and most of the spectators stared at Keith. Peter tried to fathom an ex-Catholic priest telling a sportswoman she had to be like a devil, in Heaven.

"I can see why they call this murderball," Peter said. He added this experience to his top-ten list of surreal and weird moments in the previous couple of days. "I wanted your opinion on something."

"Can't it wait till after the game? We're almost done."

"Sure."

Peter was distracted by one of Angie's teammates who had just been subbed. The player looked in his sixties — how can you tell Up Here when people can freeze their age — and had wheeled his chair out to the foyer then got up and walked to the water fountain. He's walking!

Peter ran up to him. "Hey, what are you doing?"

"Getting a drink, mate," said the player.

"Look at you, taking advantage of all these poor people. You should be ashamed of yourself."

"Mate, just back off. No one is taking advantage of anyone. We're allowed to grab a drink during the game."

"What's up guys?" asked Keith.

"What's up? Can't you see? This guy is up. He doesn't even need a wheelchair. He's a cheat."

Keith glanced back at the game then back to the guy in the wheelchair.

"Mate, no one needs a wheelchair."

Peter looked at Keith.

Keith nodded. "There aren't any disabilities Up Here; physical or mental. You still haven't read your induction information?"

He remembered Jane's full arm. "But in the Arrival Lounge I saw people in wheelchairs. I've seen them in the streets."

"You try sitting for forty years, then see how easy walking is," said the player.

"I keep bumping it all over the place," Jane had said about her new full arm.

A surge of guilt burned from his gut to his face.

"Most need quite a bit of therapy before they can walk, or use their arms, or brains normally," said Keith.

A long whistle made them all turn back to the game which had just ended. Keith made a couple of fist pumps while his players celebrated.

Angie wheeled over to them.

"So, this is part of the therapy?" asked Peter, waving his arm towards the mayhem on the court.

"Nah. This is all for fun. We love the sport so we keep playing. Angie never even had paraplegia."

"I love the violence," said Angie.

"And me. I'm Tim." He held out a hand.

"Peter," he said shaking the strongest hand he'd held.

Angie got up and kissed Tim. Peter couldn't help noticing Angie's arms were nearly as muscled as Tim's, which contrasted with her sweet voice.

"Sorry, I'm just a newbie," Peter said.

"No kidding!" said Tim.

"You should come along for a spin some time," said Angie.

"No thanks, I don't think I have the violence in me."

"A few years Up Here and you'll be back," said Angie, then laughed with Tim.

Keith led Peter to a seat. "Are you OK?"

He nodded as he watched Angie and Tim playfully spray water at each other.

"Sorry I made you miss the end of the game."

"Forget it. What's on your mind?" asked Keith.

"Seeing Jane again straight away made sense. We were together just a few months ago. It was easy. But I haven't seen Chris for over nine years. And so much has happened since then."

"Like marrying Jane."

"Exactly."

"Your hesitation makes sense to me."

"Don't you think Chris died so that I would fall in love with Jane?"

Keith let the words float around them for a few seconds. "Are you asking me, or yourself?"

Peter wasn't expecting the words thrown back at him.

"Surely, you want to see her?" Keith said. "Besides, what do you have to lose? If you're meant to be with Jane that will work itself out. But if you avoid Christina, she'll become the elephant in the room."

From his psychology studies, Peter understood how these elephants could become huge emotional beasts that trod on you when you least expected. You had to deal with them eventually or someone would get hurt. Simple in theory.

Heightened Sensations

Dying was the beginning.

Linda loosened it. Jane well and truly unscrewed the valve. Walking home from the sports center, the valve burst open and the torrent of sweet memories, emotions and torturous pain sprayed out of the Christina-container PETER had been suppressing for nine years. No matter how much processing and "moving on" he'd achieved on his own and together with Jane before he died, none of it contemplated seeing Christina again.

He staggered to a park bench, overwhelmed and underprepared. Under a deluge and in over his head. His heart projected whatever the hell it wanted onto the screen in his mind.

Memories and moments with Christina.

He took a few deep breaths, sat back and closed his eyes.

"Oh, stumbling stupids. I'm sorry," Christina mumbled into his open guitar case from her hands and knees.

PETER had just finished his busking set and she was the first to approach with some money flapping in her hand. She'd tripped, dropped her shopping bag and the lingerie she'd just bought fell into his guitar case on top of his day's takings. He helped pick up her intimate stuff.

"Usually they throw panties they're wearing, which is kinda tacky but I like new panties. Shows a bit of class. Potential I have to earn."

Christina's holiday-home smile moved into his heart and the neighborhood was never the same.

PETER was mesmerized by Christina's profile as she drove slowly, empty cans tied to the back of the car clattered along the road. Her long soft brown curls enjoyed playing with the breeze. It wasn't a battle like so many other women seemed to have with their hair. She wasn't wearing any makeup other than the red lipstick she'd borrowed from Jane for the wedding, which matched her red leather skirt and jacket. *Au naturel* was Christina's natural state. Comfortable in her skin, her clothes, her red '69 Mustang with white leather.

She turned towards him. He'd heard the phrase "touching Earth" a million times but never really understood it until he'd been grounded by Christina's smile and sparkling brown eyes. She poked her tongue out and he poked right back. They laughed in harmony, his rock-tenor tuned into her gravelly pitch.

She focused back on the road ahead as he turned to the scene behind.

A guitar case and an Esky claimed the backseat. Outside, in front of the quaint country hall, their close family and friends cried or waved or whistled. He gave them a rock salute then gripped the seat as Christina put her foot down and the Mustang squealed away on their virgin voyage as a married couple.

A few soft clouds wrestled in the hot summer sky but neither the clouds nor the tall gum tree they were shaded under provided PETER any comfort from the heat while he played his guitar. It must've been hotter for Christina as she worked on the car with grease on her face and hands, a can of beer balanced on the roof. She still sported the red leather skirt but had stripped down to her frilly red bra.

"Ooh la la, red frilly bra," he sang and strummed, "ooh la la, red frilly bra."

She'd kept her eyes off his topless body and hadn't been much of an audience; focused on her mission to get her baby purring again before the sun dropped under the horizon.

His mission was to get Christina purring.

He got up and strummed closer. He gently caressed the back of her thigh with the end of his guitar. She shivered, definitely not from cold.

He moved to the side, continuing the rhythm of his guitar.

"Rosie and Blush have come out to play," he sang.

He's the only guy who had ever nicknamed her nipples

and she's the only woman who had ever inspired a pet name for any anatomy.

"You had me when you named my nipples," she used to joke.

She grinned, picked up her beer and let some trickle out of her mouth and down her neck, converging with her sweaty cleavage. Despite the sun going down, the heat between them rose in ways a thermometer couldn't measure.

He placed his guitar against the tree. When he turned back she was shaking her can and sprayed him with beer. He retreated to the Esky, dripping wet and laughing.

Almost three years later, PETER stood in his soaking black t-shirt and jeans in the doorway of the identification and viewing room at the Melbourne Coroner's office. Glen hovered beside him, placing a wet umbrella against the wall.

An assistant opened the door but Peter couldn't step from the olive green carpet in the waiting area onto the white vinyl floor in the clinical, all-white room because at the center of the all-white room lay a body on a gurney covered by a white sheet.

Christina's body.

When the police officers had brought him the unfathomable, unimaginable news, they tried to brace him for what was to come.

They never had a chance.

He was shaking as he inched closer to the gurney. When the assistant peeled back the sheet, revealing Christina's face,

Peter's legs crumpled. Glen caught him.

"It was a big SUV," the assistant said. "She died instantly. All her injuries are below the neck and the back of her head."

The assistant's voice was distant but the only one of his senses he could bear was the vision of Christina's unscratched, unharmed face.

Perfect face.

He recovered a fraction of awareness from his nightmare and nodded towards the assistant who scribbled something on a form.

Peter collapsed over Christina. Raw waves of barbed wire ripped through him.

After what seemed like seconds, he felt Glen's hand on his shoulder. "Come on, mate. Let her rest now."

It seemed too soon. Everything with Christina seemed too soon. Every time a date ended… whenever she left the room… when she dragged her smile out of the house for work… and now…

"No, Chris… no…" The sounds barely dripped out of his lungs.

Glen gripped his other shoulder.

Peter kissed Christina's cold cheek then pushed himself up with Glen's help. The assistant covered Christina's face with the sheet, but he grabbed the assistant's arm, desperate for a fraction more time.

Lying there peacefully, even in death, Christina's face was full of life.

For a moment PETER thought Christina was doing her sloppy puppy thing, licking all over his face, but it was a big brown nose and long musky-red tongue slobbering.

"Maverick, leave the man alone. Sit."

Maverick's teenage owner pulled the big dog back and it heeled, tongue ready for more.

"Sorry," she said, "he's harmless. Must've sensed you needed some loving."

"Huge, but sensitive," said Peter, nodding.

"English mastiff. You OK?"

"Yeah, thanks." He held his hands out towards Maverick, who didn't need a second invitation. He rubbed behind its huge ears. "Thanks, big fella."

Vrooowwwwm.

Even under the Sennasation helmet he was wearing, the roar of Christina's go-kart rocked PETER every time she zoomed past him in the pits. Christina swayed through the track, sweeping around corners like she led on a dancefloor, smooth and fast, in a rhythm of her own. Her intensity simmered through the red Sennasation coveralls and yellow helmet as she pushed her kart to its G-force limits.

A Sennasation crew member checked the lap clock and did a little celebration jig. On her next pass he pointed to the electronic sign that flashed: *Track Record.*

Christina pumped her fist in the air and continued zooming around the track.

"That lap record has driven her crazy for years. Ever since

Senna set it on opening day here," said another crew member to Peter as he waited in his go-kart.

The crew member had told him the complex was all Christina's idea. She'd modelled everything on the Spa-Francorchamps circuit in Belgium because she loved the beauty of the modulating track surrounded by greenery and hills. Her hero, Ayrton Senna, attended the opening as a complete surprise.

The crew member helped start Peter's go-kart and he raced off, barely keeping control of the super-charged machine. He'd been go-karting many years ago for one of Christina's birthdays but that didn't compare with the power of this kart and the flowing track that seemed to grin at him as a challenge. He gripped the wheel tight as the track flashed past and his inner-world raced faster.

Christina quickly caught up and tried to overtake. He resisted her attempts with some shaky maneuvers, enjoying the secret moment with her on the track. It was obvious through his side mirrors that she wasn't happy, waving for him to move over.

Just as she accelerated through an inside gap, he lost control and crashed into Christina's kart, forcing both of them off the track. They glided over the gentle inner gutter and bumped their way through the grass.

His kart flew into a pile of tires, some bouncing over him, others scattering around.

Christina regained control and slid her kart to a sideways stop next to his kart. As he fumbled out of his kart, she stormed towards him, ripped down her gloves and eased off her helmet.

He was thrown back to the white sheet unveiling her face in the morgue. He stumbled back and tripped onto the tires.

"That's the only way you should be allowed on rubber," she said.

He was grateful for a few more seconds of invisibility to center himself, to take in Christina.

Christina. It's really you.

Same attention-seeking cheekbones, same cute nose and full ruby lips. Same choc-biscuit eyes. Choc-biscuit eyes that melted him. Her long curls had been dealt no favors by her helmet and the baggy coveralls were even less flattering, but he could make out her familiar curves. Christina always had a spark but it had grown into the fierce radiance of a giant bonfire.

He struggled to get out of the tires.

"You sure are one hell of a brain-dead rev-head," said Christina as she dragged him off the tires.

He fiddled with his chin strap and Christina rolled her eyes then helped unhook it. "Let me guess how you got Up Here — car accident?"

Peter yanked his helmet off. "You were nicer when this was a hobby."

Christina dropped her helmet. "Well… rev me like a Ferrari."

He'd had a little time to think about how this moment might play out, but it really wasn't something he could've prepared for. Nine years snap frozen like it was yesterday, thawed by a nuclear blast from her incendiary glare, flaming through his body to a campfire in the middle of his heart.

CHRISTINA hadn't expected Peter to just show up. She was a sweaty mess in her greasy coveralls and to make second first-appearances worse, Peter looked as simmering as ever in his usual jeans and t-shirt.

Formula One on the starting grid type of simmer.

She thought he'd call her first. They could've talked on the phone a few times before catching up. It had been a while. The phone would have been a good way to ease back into… whatever they were going to ease back into. Start with his voice then the rest. She wasn't sure whether to hug him or bang his head with the helmet.

"If your mother could see you now, she'd die," he said.

"If Mom could see me now, she'd be dead."

She smiled at how easily their banter zipped them back in time. A surge of warmth flooded through her so fast, so powerfully, it took all her strength and experience with go-kart G-forces to stay on her feet.

Peter stepped forward, arms open and she met him halfway. Nine years of pain and love and regrets smothered by one hug. His guitarist biceps felt good against her shoulders. Nice smell too, something different. Kind of lemony.

Better than my sweat-and-grease perfume.

Christina pulled back, determined to keep some semblance of control. Muddy water had settled under their nine-year bridge, and they'd need to sift it through many filters.

She followed Peter's lead with the safe subject first. "How is Mom?"

"Eleni is as strong as ever. She cooked for me after you died. Every week for a year they'd turn up with a mountain of food. Same again after my mom died. And she remembered the color and dimension of every plastic container! I was terrified I might lose one."

"Mom the Tupperware Nazi. Dad?"

"Tom's still smoking."

"Stubborn bugger."

Peter nodded. "He took your death harder than your mom, but he's OK now. Funny and grumpy, as usual."

She wiped a tear with the back of her hand. As much as she'd struggled under her parents' antiquated peasant views, with Peter providing a fresh one-degree of separation, she was looking forward to seeing them.

Peter stepped close again. "I missed you so much."

Me too.

But she couldn't say it, despite being desperate to hold him tight again, to wrestle him to the ground, touch him, kiss those soft-hard-fiery lips. Turbo-charged passion magnets.

She wrenched her eyes off his lips, picked up her helmet and gloves, threw them in her kart, then pushed it along the track.

Peter caught up with his kart. "This reminds me of the good old days pushing your old Mustang. How many times did it break down? Four, five?"

"Don't remember." She remembered every single time, but couldn't stroll down memory lane with him. Not yet.

"They were fun times. I think that old Mustang just wanted us to spend more time together."

She tried hard not to smile, angled her face away from him.

She'd always loved his corny courage, the way he spun things into a goofy romantic angle.

"At least you're grinning."

Damn.

Nine years she dreamed about this reunion but all those plans were blown up the moment Jane blurted out those three words. Now she was driving an Alpine rally track in winter without a navigator, without a map, without a steering wheel.

"So, where's Doctor Jane?" She liked the way that came out; she should remember the tone next time she needed to knock corny right off the road.

His eyes burned her cheek but she focused straight ahead.

"Chris, who knew this—?"

"I don't blame you for marrying someone, Peter. You had to get on with your life. But..." Christina stopped pushing her kart and straightened up. Peter stood tall. So tall. "Why did it have to be her?"

She could see how hard he was scrambling for the right words. His shoulders slumped and his eyes darted from her left to right eye. Usually he just zeroed in on her left. How do you remember something like that? Nine years since that muscle memory had been flexed.

"It just happened. No one—"

"It doesn't just happen. Someone makes the first move and Jane knows how to... ignite the spark plugs." Christina pushed her kart again.

Peter caught up. "We bumped into each other in Sydney."

"Sydney, how romantic."

"Chris, it was work. A psychology conference."

She pushed faster. "You don't have to explain."

If this wasn't about Jane, Jane would tell me not to give the power away to the other woman by getting angry. But this was totally about Jane so she could go and—

"I didn't see anyone for almost five years after you," Peter said as he scampered up beside her.

A hot pang of guilt slowed her down. Five years is a long time. He must really have missed her. And he's here now.

Bugger if I am going to give her control.

"It's OK, forget it."

They reached the covered pits area, parked the karts then she headed into the workshop. She sensed her new Peter-shadow but focused on putting tools away.

"We can't change what's happened, Chris. Please don't be angry."

"I'm not angry but I've got stuff to do before closing."

She was surprised at the anger simmering, and disappointed it had snuck through. She'd grown heaps in the last nine years, no question, especially since opening Sennasation. She'd been cruising on her path and never expected the oil slick dropped by Jane.

"I married Peter."

Not in a million meditations would she have seen that coming. Three months since that night and her heart and mind were still slipping and crashing.

She picked up an oil can from the floor next to a kart and headed for the bench.

"Before you died, I can't remember one negative moment," said Peter.

She fiddled with parts and tools on the bench. It was true; two years dating, three years of marriage and she couldn't remember one argument. Everything had been so cruisy with Peter.

He stood in front of her. Her soul wanted to jump into his arms again, her spirit strengthened defensive resistance; a hopeless internal stalemate.

His eyes caressed every millimeter of her face. She'd missed the way he did that, like he was gently laying her down on a cloud of cotton.

"You didn't stop your aging," he said.

"I think we just had a negative moment." She tried to walk around Peter but he blocked her.

"No, no, you look stunning."

She wiped her free hand on her coveralls a couple of times.

"Well, with a shower and clean clothes you'd be stunning."

She squirted oil on Peter's t-shirt.

He jumped back. "Hey! Is that 'oil' you got?"

She squirted him again. "That's for the pathetic gag."

This time Peter didn't flinch. "Were you waiting for me?"

Cheeky monkey.

She waved the oil can in front of Peter. "Obviously your ego doesn't need any lubrication."

No way was she going to give him the satisfaction of the truth. There was a lot of servicing and parts to check in the engine of their relationship before she was ready for that. Maybe the engine was unfixable. They don't build emotional engines in a workshop with tools neatly lined up.

She placed the oil can on the bench. "I know it's all weird. None of us could have expected this." Her gaze concentrated on the tool panel to the right of his head. Easier that way.

Peter shook his head.

"Least of all an apathetic atheist," she added. An apathetic atheist who taught her so much about herself. Who Christina had grown to love more as she got to know her soul better and found her true path Up Here.

Then he went and spoiled it all by marrying Doctor Jane.

"Chris, I don't know how we're all going to work this out, I really don't. If you have any ideas, I'm all ears."

She finally met his eyes. Big puppy-brown eyes. She had no idea either. She was still grappling with the conversation with Jane. Those five words shattered a nine-year dream laced with hope and longing. With Peter in front of her, the dream and confusion simultaneously magnified.

Cars are much easier. You find the problem, fix it. Drive on.

She shook her head gently and shrugged.

"I do know I'd like to see you again… without the oil can," said Peter.

She looked at him, at the oil can, then back at Peter. Of course she wanted to see him again. Jane wasn't going to win this without a fight.

"OK, but no more surprises. I'll call you."

"Soon?"

"Soon enough." Nothing wrong with making him sweat a little.

"Good ol' mystery o'clock," said Peter, smiling.

She couldn't resist smiling at the flashback. She had always been elusive with time and committing to dates, especially in their early days. Peter coined the phrase back then hoping to jolt her out of the habit. Some things don't change.

"Yeah, see you at mystery o'clock."

Married. To Peter. Crazy! Yet Christina Christian had a synergy to it.

From the moment CHRISTINA walked into the old country hall, Peter's smile had been on high-beam all day. In his vintage black suit with shiny lapels, black shirt and thin red leather tie, he looked like a classic muscle car.

She snuck another peek at Peter's glistening upper body as she pushed her Mustang from the driver's door with one hand and steered with the other. Peter, beside the "Just Married" sign, pushed from the back, his guitarist guns taught, revving her insides like a Ferrari.. Their jackets and Peter's shirt made love on the backseat. She was jealous.

She'd been sure the niggly engine gremlins were sorted before their big day but her beloved Mustang was a fickle beast. Her pride and joy had spluttered to a halt ten kilometers short of the cottage she'd booked for the first few nights of their honeymoon. Not having a lot of money was never going to stop her planning a fun road trip.

The first two times CHRISTINA had just hung at the back; Peter always drew a decent crowd to his lunchtime busking sessions since he'd set up near the boatshed café a week after Christmas. Catching glimpses through arms and over shoulders his presence smoldered from his eyes, through his fingers and guitar strings, oozing out of his little amplifier and teased every pore of her body.

No more getting a young kid to drop money in his guitar case for her. This time she stood at the front and was going to walk right up and say, "Hi, I'm Christina, and I was wondering what other gigs you had."

"Gigs" was the cool word to slip in.

Hooley bedooleys, he's playing my favorite Angels song, Am I Ever Gonna See Your Face Again.

A fireworks factory exploded in her heart, she'd never heard it performed the way Doc Neeson had meant it — as a beautiful aching ballad — and in hindsight, that was probably the moment she'd fallen in love with Peter. The crowd went crazy and she stepped forward, steady and casual, reaching him before he'd unstrapped his guitar.

And tripped. Like a seventeen year-old drunken teenager on a spring break, ending on her hands and knees with her head over his guitar case like she was going to vomit. That would've been less mortifying than being a twenty-six year-old klutz. Vomiting might've got a bit of sympathy. She hid under her hair; for once the recalcitrant jungle of curls was useful.

Oh God, my lingerie.

Her brand new lingerie had spilled from her shopping bag into his guitar case. Like a hopeless groupie. She had to fight to stifle a scream because her knickers were in his guitar case and a scream would have topped off the whole groupie thing.

She stayed face down while she tried to compose herself and think of something brilliant to say.

And then he said that corny line, with those eyes doing a light show and she was the only one on his stage.

"Christiiina... Hey, boss lady."

CHRISTINA snapped out of Peter-Music-Land to see George waving his hand in front of her face.

"You OK?" he asked.

"Yeah, sure. I was just thinking about some track changes."

"Aha. Nothing to do with that ex-husband dropping by?" he asked with a shiny Chevy grin.

"Nothing to do you with your business, George."

"Got it. You right to close up?"

She nodded.

"See ya in the fast lane," he said heading for the gate.

"Hey, George."

He turned around.

"Next time you call me boss lady, make sure you add a 'Ma'am' and a salute at the end."

"Yes, ma'am," he said, and then added a lazy salute to his grin.

Walking home, PETER found it hard to believe the fiery rocket of a woman was once a demure flower in her parents' tightly-controlled garden. The good Greek girl who made her gardeners proud by blossoming into a pristine teacher, while all the time she craved a greasy independence.

Christina had loved cars and working on cars, as if her subconscious wanted to build something to drive her away from the claustrophobic garden. He sensed her inner spark when they first met. He'd encouraged her transition and it was a slow burn. But Up Here she had become her own woman. It only made her more compelling; something he never would have dreamed possible.

And she didn't stop her ageing. There's only one reason she made that decision: him. That's a good sign.

Mystery o'clock.

He laughed with the trees at the throwback to their early dating. Mystery o'clock was probably more relevant than ever.

"After the sugar hit there's the crunchy outer layer, then the contrasting texture of the gooey dough."

PETER couldn't believe that Keith had never tried Spanish donuts. Keith took another bite and his smile wrestled with his chewing motion. Then his pupils narrowed, skin glowed.

"Yes, yes. Just when you thought it couldn't get any better, the jam inundates your senses. What a rush, hey?"

Sitting on his usual wooden crate in his usual lane at the Vic Market, Peter's mouth watered so much it felt like a swamp.

Keith chewed a little quicker then ravaged another bite, nodding like a clown.

Peter pulled a donut out of his own bag and munched half in one bite.

"Performing live, making love and Spanish jam donuts. My favorite three rushes," said Peter in between chews.

"Well, I can claim one out of three now," said Keith.

He stopped chewing and stared at Keith, who realized the major confession he'd inadvertently made. Keith pulled out another donut and took a big bite, his cheeks redder than the thick donut jam.

Of course, he'd been a priest till late in his life. The guy's a virgin.

Peter's first instinct was to make a joke out of it but it didn't feel right. Somehow their roles had reversed and he was the one receiving the intimate information at this unlikely confessional. He looked around for some inspiration. The market was mostly the same but bigger and part of it a little more vintage. A group of elderly male stall workers, maybe owners, laughed loud as they enjoyed a coffee break down the lane.

"What's said at the market, stays at the market," Peter said.

Keith glanced at him and nodded with a sheepish smile more teenage virgin than worldly virgin.

They enjoyed their donuts people-watching for a while.

"How did it go with Christina?" said Keith.

"Crazy. Sweet. Fun. Bit awkward when she brought up Jane but I felt good when I walked home. Still do."

"Good for you."

"I feel so lucky. Like we've just had the high school dance and I get to date the joint prom-Queen winners."

Keith nodded. "Well, you never actually divorced or broke up with either of them, so there's nothing wrong with spending time with both."

"Yeah, I guess. Although it's hard to not think about getting more intimate with both of them." He looked at Keith. "Is that so wrong for me to think, let alone say?"

"As a wise man once said to me, what's said at the market stays at the market."

Laughter burst out of Peter. Keith caught the bug too.

After a while, they raised their donut bags and touched them together in a toast.

PETER had knocked over a beer at home. Not knocked over as in skolled; knocked over as in spilled onto the floor, sprayed onto his socks and splashed onto the bottom of his jeans. So he dressed twice, along with brushing his teeth twice, because he was never sure if he'd brushed them the first time.

First date-itis. The never-mentioned disease amongst otherwise healthy, functional adults. Kind of embarrassing, because not only wasn't it a first date, it was a date with his wife. Jane.

"I didn't say I'd rather not come but of all the things we could be doing, looking at an exhibition of dead artists wasn't top of my list," said Peter as they arrived at the Heide Museum of Modern Art, Jane's favorite place in Melbourne.

"It's not an exhibition, Peter," Jane said. "This is a demonstration by dead artists."

"Oh, yeah… that's different."

An eclectic crowd lined up in the Heide III foyer and courtyard. Although, for this type of event it probably was normal. He could have predicted the Melbourne-black clothes with splashes of colorful scarves, even though it was warm. The hats, goatee beards amongst bushranger beards and the "don't look at me, but I am different" boots shuffling forward on women and men.

"Have I told you that you look delicious?" he said.

Jane's black singlet top felt silky when he'd greeted her, while her tight patterned black pants showed off her long legs without showing much at all. The only sign that she may have gone to any trouble was the red lipstick.

"Three times."

She rolled her eyes but he caught the briefest of curls on her lips before she pointed to the rear of the main room. "Over there."

⁓

JANE led Peter to a solid round stand about a foot high at the back of the room. She stepped up and he snuggled in behind her. There was definitely some kind of unauthorized melting inside her. The heat off his arms and hands over her stomach turned the simmering which had begun earlier into a sizzle.

Focus, Jane. Amazing artists. This is a rare treat.

Through the huge glass viewing wall two male and two female artists worked in a large studio. The banners above the artists read: *SIDNEY NOLAN, SUNDAY REED, ALBERT TUCKER, JOY HESTER.*

Every now and then Sunday Reed joined Sidney Nolan, took his brush and dabbed on his painting. Sidney approved; the two of them seemed to have a special bond. His painting looked like one of his classics, Ned Kelly in Australian bushland, except in this one he was holding hands with a woman in Arab dress wearing a black burqa. She was drawn to this stunning vision because the burqa looked uncannily similar to Ned Kelly's distinctive armor.

"That's brilliant," Jane said, pointing to the painting.

"Yeah. We can copy it at the next fancy dress party."

She didn't encourage him with a reaction but couldn't help smiling. She snuggled back into him. The Peter-date nerves earlier were annoying. She went through three tops, two skirts, a dress and finally the pants before heading off tonight. He's the only guy that had ever affected her like that. The only constant and easy decision was the lipstick; a stamp that usually ended up smudged all over his mouth, face, neck. The red vision flared through her.

"Apparently sex Up Here is amazing," said Peter.

He's reading my mind!

"Apparently," Jane said, trying to keep a smooth voice.

"Everything is heightened."

She grinned and tightened her arms around his. It's not like their sexual connection needed heightening, but the thought zinged through her body.

"Have you thought about moving in again?"

She shook her head and focused back on the painters. This wasn't the time to drag Peter to a secluded room and ignite their heightened reunion. Zing, zing, zing.

"I saw Christina yesterday."

The zinging zanged. "And?"

"She's as spicy as ever."

Jane wasn't surprised. Christina's love-appease-hate-rebel-love pattern with her parents created a layer of anger that sometimes seeped out as passive-aggressive behavior.

"But I think it's going to be OK. I think we can do this as adults," Peter said before nuzzling her neck. "I can't wait till we can be adults…"

"Mmm…"

"I'm seeing her again tomorrow."

A cold flush surged through her, like a fierce spray from a firetruck hose in the middle of an icy winter.

She stepped off the little stand, right through Peter's closed arms. Peter lost his balance and stumbled.

The shock on his face scared her as much as her instinctive reaction. She knew about the principle Up Here that a soul could never be held against its will. A brilliant phenomena she'd wished could've existed for all the vulnerable souls on Earth. She never imagined needing to do it Up Here. Walking right through Peter's arms discombobulated her sense of control, her very essence.

All of the Peter she knew drained from his face. No sparkly eyes, no cheeky grin, no color in his cheeks. It compounded the confusion swirling inside her head, desperately searching for a logical reason she'd walked right through his arms.

She scurried out of the room.

⌇

PETER caught up with Jane in the foyer.

"What was that? How did you do that? How did you walk right through my arms?"

"A soul can't be held against its will."

"Against your will?"

"It's an instinctive thing. Protective."

"Protective? You died in these arms."

"Did Christina ever die in your heart?" Spiky question marks flew out of her eyes into his gut.

Pain ripped through his body. He wasn't sure if it was still the shock at how Jane walked through his arms, or disappointment at what she'd said, or guilt. Because deep down in his soul, he wasn't certain he could give Jane the answer she'd want to hear.

When it came to navigating the tricky roads of heightened sensations and emotions, he was still wearing L-plates. He'd read the positives of the hyper-sensitivity far outweighed the negatives, however, right then, he was buried under hyper-confusion and frustration.

Jane rubbed her hands up and down the side of her thighs, head on that angle, with a deep furrowed brow. He couldn't remember one moment in the last three or four years where she was lost for words; where the world didn't seem to orbit around her.

Then Jane shambled outside. That's twice she'd walked away.

Couldn't remember that either.

Gelato in a Bowl

JANE had never run from anything.

Her surgeon father and magazine editor mother were proud of the intellectual fighter they'd molded. Their dinner table witnessed a constant three-way war of words and ideals. That's why the real world never phased her; yet Up Here, her emotions increasingly overpowered her brain. She felt like a foreigner in her own body, exacerbated by guilt for the pain and fear she'd created in Peter.

Shuffling around the sculptures in Heide's gardens helped balance her. Fresh air, sun, art; she needed all the help she could get. She was also grateful Peter had stayed with her and walked in silence. Two rosellas swooped past them as they chased each other from tree to tree, perching at a bench before they flew off again.

"You know, Jane, whatever this situation is, we're equally responsible."

She nodded, noting his somber, vulnerable timbre.

Apart from her cancer, the few moments in her life that she felt out of control were all created by Peter. Mostly she was thankful for his persistent shaking of her comfort-tree and secretly enjoyed the fruits of playful romance that fell from her tight branches. But she wasn't proud of lashing out at him inside the gallery. It forced her to accept that her feelings for Peter hadn't changed just because she, Peter and Christina were all together now.

Being passive wasn't going to lead them down a clearer path, nor was it in her DNA.

"About moving in…"

"Yes?" Peter's tone sparked up.

"What if we do it in stages?"

"You mean like a couple of nights a week?"

Her inner-world morphed from a shaky steel coil to a steady sweet smile at his eternal optimism and instant unspoken forgiveness. "I really miss painting. Do you mind if I set up my stuff in your garage again?"

"I'd like that." He opened and closed his arms. "Can you promise to never do that thing again?"

"I'll try. But imagine if we could do that on Earth… how many men, women and children wouldn't have to suffer if a soul couldn't be held against their will."

Peter nodded.

She opened her arms wide.

He exaggerated hesitation with a furrowed brow and squinting eyes. She smiled. He stepped towards her and they hugged. She was sure Peter felt the same surge of relief she did.

He kissed her forehead, lips warm, gentle, unrushed. It melted away her remaining tension.

When she opened her eyes the Caravaggio-Pixar Peter was back, eyes sparkling. She took his arm and they followed the winding path. Maybe the two trees ahead were an omen, the way the old trunks and high branches leant on each other, creating an evergreen arch-portal to a private patch, overlooking a sweeping bend of the Yarra River.

"Remember how you used to hide between the shrubs or behind the big pots and ornaments? Always took me ages to find you."

PETER followed Linda's gaze across the busy balcony tables. Beasley's Tea House must have been one of the first nurseries to add a café way before the spelling of "coffee" had changed to "Melbourne". It was his mom's go-to spot even when she could barely scrape the coins together for his milkshake. He definitely didn't appreciate what a pretty spot it was when he was a kid. But he was there on a non-gardening mission.

"Yes, Mom, grand memories. But who's hiding now?"

She concentrated hard on her Scotch finger biscuit, broke it in half down the middle. He could never do that without breaking the damn thing into four pieces. Then she dunked the half-biscuit into her milky tea. She was testing his patience but he respected her sweet-tooth ritual and let her enjoy biting into the soggy biscuit. He chopped off a piece of his ridiculously good chocolate-raspberry brownie with a fork and chewed to ten.

"You're avoiding Jane's calls."

"I'm not avoiding her calls." She avoided his eyes. "I've

been busy in the shop. Aren't those Japanese maples a gorgeous color?"

"You had time for my call and this."

She shifted in her seat, fiddled with the straps on her handbag then faced him. "Alright, enough with the psychologist tone. I'll call her. We'll catch up."

"And you'll keep an open mind? Try and enjoy it?"

She nodded.

"Thanks, Mom. I really believe you two will get on." He devoured the rest of the brownie.

"God knows what we'd talk about," she said.

Shoe shopping.

JANE was surprised by Linda's suggestion. It wasn't how she expected her first solo encounter with Peter's mom to play out but it made sense. Both Jane's and Linda's go-to girl for most things social, Christina, was in her own parallel fashion universe and couldn't be dragged near a shoe store.

The magnetism of shopping for shoes was a mystery to men and that's how women liked it. She loved the hunt, the stalking, the special find which slipped onto her feet like a natural extension. Maybe there was a Cinderella glass-slipper magic at its core. She knew some women loved imagining themselves strutting through a herd of men on heels that could attract any one of them, or spear right through their thick ego. The addiction of shoe shopping satiated on so many levels.

She met Linda on the corner of Greville and Izzet. Another surprise. Jane loved this pocket of the independent fashion world in Prahran, so close but a world away from much of the commercial fare in nearby Chapel St. She never would have picked Linda as a regular in this pioneer of casual cafes, boutique designers and fashion warehouses in grungy lanes.

She had no doubt Linda's motives were the same as hers: they were only doing this for Peter, a simple mutual mission. Just as well because there were few words exchanged at their awkward air kiss greeting. Linda had quickly guided the conversation onto the safe subject of shoes and led them into a lane Jane barely recognized.

There was a bazaar setup as far as she could see; colored stalls showing off clothing racks, handmade jewelry, bags and other accessories. Rectangular stripy umbrellas were interspersed with the unmistakable round umbrellas covering tables at el fresco cafes and the teasing aroma of coffee, cakes and pastries.

They had to stop as a crowd broke out in spontaneous dance to music blaring from one of the cafes. This was the third time Jane had witnessed this phenomena Up Here. She'd discussed this with other psychologists Up Here. People seemed to have shed the layers hiding their natural spirits, layers which the grind and social norms on Earth had entrenched over centuries. Everyone was more comfortable being themselves and the energy was infectious. If people felt like dancing or singing in public, they did. Rather than scoff or ridicule them, others were more likely join in or clap along.

When the singing and dancing ended they stepped into the wide entrance of Beth Levine Shoes, Jane's eyes widened. The sheer magnitude of the store struck her, yet the vibrant design filled it with a fun and friendly vibe. There seemed to be as many staff as customers, wearing colorful t-shirts emblazoned with either "Shoe Dreamer" or "Foot Angel".

The store was broken up into unique sections; specialty boutiques offering a massive range of footwear and creative displays. Each boutique featured plush recliner armchairs with individual screens jutting from the arm, like a first class airline seat.

Jane was so mesmerized with the whole experience, she hadn't noticed they'd been sat down in armchairs in the boot section until Linda tapped her arm.

"Beth Levine broke through the men's world of fashion design in the fifties. Can you imagine how tough she was to achieve that? Back in those days she had to set up her brand under her husband's name, Herbert Levine. Up Here everything is in her name and this is her magic."

"Didn't she design those amazing white boots Nancy Sinatra wore for *These Boots Are Made for Walking*"? Jane said.

"She did indeed. And Streisand's boots in *Funny Girl*"

"Really?" Jane admired Streisand's shattering of glass ceilings. A courageous pioneer, Streisand was not only a movie star but also one of the first women to produce and direct movies. All while she ran a lazy side business of being one of the most successful singers in the world.

"Beth also custom designed shoes for Marilyn and Jackie," said Linda.

"Two pairs of shoes slipped under the President's bed, by two different women, made by the same designer."

They laughed. Linda pressed a button on Jane's armchair and within seconds, a male Foot Angel knelt down in front of her. She was surprised when the Foot Angel took off her shoe and massaged her foot. His dreamy physique made the most of the stretchiness in his t-shirt, yet his hands were so gentle.

She looked at Linda and couldn't help giggling. Maybe Linda had an ulterior motive bringing her here? Who cares! This is heaven. Since sore feet weren't an issue Up Here, this only helped prove that massage was good for the soul.

"If there is a God, she must be a woman," she said.

Linda laughed. As bubbly and infectious as Peter's, an octave or two higher. Linda hit a button on her chair and a Shoe Dreamer glided over. Linda asked for the Sinatra white stiletto boots. He was back in a minute, having picked her size just from looking at her feet. The Shoe Dreamer worked them over Linda's tight jeans then filmed her walking back and forth in the boots.

Linda got comfy in her chair again and turned to Jane. "Watch this. Funky bar," she said into her screen.

A video came up showing people enjoying cocktails at a bar swathed in crimson velvet, baroque lounges and chandeliers. Onscreen, Linda appeared at the entrance then swayed through the crowded bar, with men drooling and women envious as they ogled at her stunning Sinatra boots.

It wasn't the technology which amazed her — all of it was available on Earth — but this dreamy experience was surely created by women, for women.

"You look amazing," said Jane.

"Thank you."

She didn't think real bonding was going to be a part of the agenda. She had leaned on words like "duty", "necessity" and, "Stay calm, you're doing this for Peter" in her self-talk to prepare for the potentially disastrous catch up. But she liked Linda.

Linda placed a hand on hers. "I never embraced my femininity on Earth. Sexiness wasn't encouraged and career was a foreign word in the suburbs."

"Some of my modern sisters don't appreciate the struggles in your era."

"Era… makes me sound like a dinosaur."

"Sorry I didn't mean—"

Linda patted her hand, a twinkle in her eye. "It didn't take a few public successes like Beth Levine, or Streisand, or Madonna to shatter those glass ceilings. If we all didn't push up from the bottom, those famous women wouldn't have been able to break through at the top. I guess that opened opportunities for all of you."

"And we appreciate it." She squeezed Linda's hand.

Linda squeezed right back.

They admired her white boots, a symbol of women not just walking but marching through male trenches and fences.

"You can't think of one, can you?" said Christina.
She'd been talking about how equality and diversity weren't issues Up Here, how no-one questioned her dream to build and run Sennasation; then she flipped the usual thought process challenging PETER to come up with areas or skills where men had outgrown or caught up with women in recent times.

"Typing," Peter said, relieved he'd come up with an answer.

"Typing?"

"Because we grow up with computers now, men under

forty are just as fast or faster typists than women. Most men never used to type in the old days."

"That's it? Typing?"

"In the last fifty years, that's the only thing I can think of where men have gained on women."

"Here's a little secret, Pete — we're not too fussed about that one." Christina chuckled and shook her head. "Typing."

He didn't mind being the target of Christina's amusement. From their earliest days there was never an edge to it, not a hint of aggressiveness or defensiveness in any of their exchanges. More importantly, he never needed to impress Christina.

They ambled side by side, sandwiched between the Yarra River and Alexandra Gardens. On one side the colored lights from the water fountain shimmered in the distance. Across the river, the attention-seeking neon lights of the city and landmark design of Federation Square were alive with the hum of nocturnal play.

Christina's loose summer dress fluttered with the warm breeze. Her Grecian sandals, with leather straps above her ankles, seemed the only attempt at dressing up her usual choice of flip-flops.

They gravitated towards a colorful busker playing the violin on stilts in a Carmen Miranda-inspired costume outside the Boatshed Cafe. They only caught the end of the show and as the crowd dispersed, the significance of the location hit Peter.

"This is where we met."

Christina smiled.

He'd never planned a destination. They'd started talking outside her Richmond apartment and over the next ninety minutes had ended here where they met twelve years ago.

"You accidently spilt your shopping in my guitar case," he said.

"Who said it was an accident?" Her grin simultaneously gorgeous and mischievous.

He was convinced that women were always three steps ahead when it came to potential sex or romance but had never considered their chance meeting wasn't a complete accident. He smiled and shrugged.

"It's a pity you gave up on your band," said Christina.

"After you and Mom died I just couldn't get on stage again. I had no idea what to do with my degree. I certainly didn't want to work as a clinical psychologist. When Glen offered the partnership it was an easy decision."

"You don't miss it?"

"I miss performing."

"I don't miss teaching. I love what I do now. Do you still write?"

"I started a few songs but never really finished any."

His music died when Christina did but he didn't want to dump a guilt trip on her. Or maybe he didn't want to admit he gave up at a critical time; just as their manager had a deal on the table from Merger Music. He has read since how common it is for many talented artists or athletes to find a way to fail, essentially quit, on the verge of success.

He pointed to the little a-frame poster. "Gelato?"

"Sure."

"I'll get them. What flavor?"

"The usual."

"Right… the usual."

"I'll get a table."

CHRISTINA loved the warmth smoldering inside her. After all these years, all the grieving and pain. The hundreds of hours of work it took to reach acceptance of being Up Here without Peter, moving on… and now there he was, at their favorite place in the world, looking so rock star in jeans and black t-shirt. The whole night had been Cadillac cruisy. Maybe things would work out after all, despite everything that had happened since.

Easy girl. Go with the flow.

Peter headed back with two cold bowls and one hot body. "What are you grinning about?"

"Nothing," she pointed at one of the bowls. "You still stuck on chocolate and coffee?"

"*Mais oui.* And for you *mademoiselle*, we have the finest, most exquisite chocolate and strawberry. *Et voilà.*"

Smoldering warmth turned as cold as the gelato. She looked up, struggling to reconcile the love in his eyes with his obvious betrayal.

"Have I stuffed up?"

Massive understatement.

"Strawberry is Jane's favorite." She'd tried to say the words with a nonchalant tone, but they came out as nonchalant-flavored icicles.

Peter looked mortified, holding a hand over his stomach.

Good, he deserves to suffer a little.

"Be right back," said Peter.

"Don't bother, I'm don't feel like it now."

But he'd already zipped halfway to the kiosk.

She stared at the bowl and the couples around her. To forget her favorite flavor is one thing, but to confuse it with Jane's is unforgivable.

This was a big mistake. He's with Jane now. I should leave.

But she didn't; she didn't know what to do. Cadillac-cruisy had rolled and ended on its roof.

Peter scampered back with a scoop of mango gelato in a bowl.

"Chocolate and mango. How could I forget?" Peter used a spoon to take the chocolate gelato out of Christina's bowl and placed it in the new bowl with mango. *"Et voilà."*

She couldn't remember a time when his face looked so strawberry.

She scooped up the strawberry gelato with a spoon.

"For our next trick, we will show how three flavors can magically fit into one bowl."

She poured the strawberry gelato on top of the chocolate and mango in her bowl. The strawberry slowly slid off the bowl onto the table.

"Et voilà." She glared at him.

His eyes studied the messy gelato then slinked back up to hers. His lips moved like he was about to say something, but nothing came out. Negative moments between them were becoming common.

Maybe things would have played out like this anyway. They were young, virtually in their honeymoon phase. All couples start fighting, don't they? Drifting apart? Nine years is a long time. Maybe his tastes had evolved. He's not even a muso anymore. She would never have picked that, not in a million meditations. She also tried hard to ignore the idea that

Peter may be more comfortable with Jane, but couldn't help staring at the strawberry gelato. She threw a napkin over it and looked for refuge at the Yarra.

A small soggy log floated down the dark river, spinning and turning at the mercy of a current it couldn't control.

Base Jumping

"Your favorite singer is David Bowie."

Peter's voice sounded tinny through the speaker on her phone but CHRISTINA still detected his higher pitch. Bowie was playing on her sound system in the lounge; he probably could hear it in the background. She continued painting her toenails, hunched on top of a towel on her bed. It was something she'd planned to do before seeing Peter earlier that night but time always evaporates pre-date. "Mystery o'clock" turns into "vacuum o'clock". Post gelato-fiasco, she'd needed a little self-love so her toenails received caressing attention.

"Too easy," she said.

She almost hadn't answered when Peter rang but was glad she did. It was fun hearing him squirm, besides, a splash of playful punishment was the least he deserved. He must have called as soon as he got home. He claimed he was desperate to prove he remembered her intimately and hadn't forgotten all her flavors and idiosyncrasies.

"You use chunky tomatoes to make Bolognese… and your secret ingredient is honey."

Christina yawned loudly.

"In winter you always wore light brown flannelette pajamas with the little blue teddy bears in circles."

She smiled. She still had those old pajamas Up Here. More than a little tattered, she'd taken them into Sennasation to use as rags but could never relegate them to the greasy task so they gathered dust on a hook next to her tools. For a moment her mind drifted back to toasting marshmallows on the fire at Peter's place, both in their pajamas, Peter strumming on his guitar…

"You're smiling, aren't you?" he said.

"You've forgotten gloating isn't one of my favorite colors."

Silence for a moment. She'd hit a little bullseye.

"You paint all your toes a different color and your big toe is always pink."

Her nail polish brush, dipped in hot pink, hovered in the air.

Peter's phone intimacy launched waves of warmth through her again. Damn these heightened sensations! It's much easier to be tough without the emotional gates swinging wide open all the time.

"Enough with the squirming," she said.

"Apology lunch tomorrow. Pick you up at twelve."

"No." Christina put her nail brush back in the pink bottle and stared at the sky through the window.

How is avoiding him going to help? What are you afraid of?

The stars weren't reflecting any answers. David Bowie nudged her with his haunting *Where Are We Now?*

"I'll pick you up. Eleven-ish," she said.

"I'll be ready."

"Arrroooo… arrrooo…"

PETER did his best impersonation of a howling dog as they roared down the highway in Christina's funky beach buggy.

"You OK?" she said.

"Like a dog in a Ute."

Finally her smile cracked through, magnifying the glow in her eyes like pilot lights, always flickering, firing up the kindle in his heart.

"I'm so lucky we don't need sunglasses Up Here," he said.

She snapped her head forward again.

He chuckled. Christina lived her emotions, Hell, she ran five miles ahead of her emotions. Her phony nonchalance was never going to last the three-hour drive. Her long wavy hair shimmied like golden-brown streamers under the early afternoon sun. It threw him back to their wedding day in her beloved Mustang.

"You're missing the scenery," she said, eyes on the road.

Got all the scenery I need…

"Arrrooo… arrrooo…"

And there it was, the second sunrise for the day blazing from her smile. Without looking at him, she pushed his face towards the road. When her hand went back to the steering wheel, he snuck a quick glance. She was still smiling.

Mission accomplished

The scenery as they approached the high country near Bright had always been beautiful but he sensed something different.

"Do we have some kind of super-vision now?"

"Context?"

He gripped the door and dash for balance as she zoomed around a sweeping s-bend.

"Every color seems more intense, even the shadows are sharper."

"No pollution," she said.

"Wow, that's incredible."

Christina nodded. "We do have 20-20 vision now, but the magic is in the pure environment."

He was born into a world with pollution and greenhouse gasses, and it obviously got worse each year of his life. In hindsight, it was embarrassing how easy it was to get used to.

"How can they possibly turn an environmental ship with seven billion passengers around to this purity on Earth?"

"Not by doing nothing."

Classic Chris nugget.

"Hang on," she said.

He braced himself again as she swung her shiny red buggy into a BP service station. Using the brakes was optional for Christina and it felt like they glided in on two wheels.

When the buggy stopped, an army of service assistants trotted over like a grand prix racing team, only less intimidating. Two wiped the windscreen, one checked under the bonnet and two others checked the tires. An elderly looking guy with long thick grey hair dawdled over and plugged in a charging cable.

"You look as gorgeous as ever, Christina. Full charge" he said.

"Thanks, Stan. Yes, please. We're heading up the mountain."

"Are all cars electric?" asked Peter.

Christina nodded and pointed to the roof of the service station.

"All glass on all buildings are solar panels. And there are invisible solar panels on all west-facing walls. The transparent lining helps insulate the building and creates power."

"And this is what BP does now?"

"They are Tesla's biggest distributor Up Here. How are BP doing on Earth?"

"Not so good."

Another car pulled in and another army jumped out to spoil it.

"Heaven to Peter… are you OK?"

He smiled and squeezed Christina's arm. "Yes, very OK. I was just appreciating things Up Here a little more." He lingered on her eyes.

She pointed at the mountain. "Ready for an adventure?"

"So, we're going on a secluded picnic?"

Christina shook her head.

"A bush walk?"

"All done. Have fun," said Stan, giving Christina a slow wink.

"Thanks, Stan. We will," she replied with an exaggerated wink.

"Why are you two winking like that?"

Christina grinned then hit the accelerator. He braced himself as she swung the buggy back onto the highway. Her grin could lead him into any dark alley. Any unchartered waters. He'd follow that grin anywhere.

"No way," PETER said, embarrassed with the high pitch.

He couldn't believe people were walking or running to the edge of a cliff and jumping off. *Without* parachutes. His body tightened like over-tuned electric guitar strings. Standing with Christina near the back of a level grassed area nestled into the mountain, the scenery was spectacular; but all Peter could see were stupid people jumping off a cliff.

"This is base jumping in its purest form. You'll love it, Pete."

So tense, his head shook like a robot. He remembered watching Glen paragliding years ago. He couldn't get used to the idea of him and his mates walking off a cliff then, even with specially designed parachutes and months of training. This was crazier.

"You can't hurt yourself. It's all mental."

"Absolutely mental," he said.

"Just watch for a while."

Christina held his arm and guided him to the viewing platform built over the edge.

A harmony of panic made him turn back to the runway. Four friends ran together, holding hands, screaming louder as they neared the edge. They jumped off and let go in the air, performing coordinated rolls and spins before thudding onto the grass nine hundred yards below. Like a child studying an ant farm, he watched them on the ground. They got up, dusted themselves off and high-fived, before running to the nearby chairlift.

Next on the runway he recognized Dawn, his co-arrival Up Here. She skipped towards the edge singing Doris Day's *Whatever Will Be Will Be* as she leaped off with an energetic dive, glided down, spinning in controlled tumble rolls before landing with a belly flop.

"If she can do it, you can, Pete."

"Forget it, Chris. You go, I'll watch."

"I bet once you do your first base jump, you'll be straight back up for another go." She extended a hand to shake.

He moved both his hands away, still shaking his head.

"Together." Christina placed her palm up. "Please?" She molded her face into a cute puppy-dog look.

He couldn't ever remember saying no to Christina. The few times he might have been close melted away as soon as he saw that face. If he listed all the reasons why he married Christina, this exaggerated silly look would be top-five. He'd never been with any other woman who was confident enough in herself to not care how silly she may appear. The raw vulnerability of showing how much something meant to her in the moment was irresistible.

He looked at her hand, then the cliff edge. He had to trust her. He also didn't want to look like a wimp. There was no logic to his fear. He was dead.

I'm a soul and I can't feel physical pain.

"What the hell, let's do it."

Christina held his hand tight and jogged to the beginning of the runway with his arm dragging behind. She swung him around and kept moving, not giving him a chance to stop and back out. They built up speed and when they jumped off the edge, she let go of his hand.

He screamed with terror. Christina shrieked with thrill.

He floated down for a few seconds. When he opened his eyes, Christina was gliding through controlled tumbles and spins.

Thump!

He bounced off the cliff face like a rag doll all the way down and finished spread-eagled on his back.

CHRISTINA ran over and stood over Peter.

He opened one eye slowly, then the other. Moved one arm, then the other.

"I'm OK! Unbelievable. I'm OK."

She helped him up.

"That was wow-mazing!" His eyes burned with excitement.

Peter picked her up and spun her around. She shrieked, partly relieved with Peter's breakthrough joy, partly deep in her own euphoria. When Peter set her down, she didn't want to let go. His face close, on so many levels this was the closest they had been in more than nine years.

An intoxicating warmth gushed through her, a sweetness and power she had never felt. Peter edged in for a kiss. She had missed his lips and their slow passionate kisses more than anything. But she couldn't, not then. Not yet. It took all her emotional strength to walk through Peter's arms.

"Come on, let's go again before it gets crowded."

Peter glared at his arms. "I hate that." He beat each arm with the opposite hand. "Man up, you two!"

She sprinted towards the chairlift before the desire to drag Peter behind the nearby trees overcame her. Peter slapped her bottom as he ran past. She was glad her walk-through hadn't upset him but wasn't going to let him get away with slapping her. Just as they were about to sit on the moving chair, she pushed it back and Peter hit the ground. She giggled so hard she had to let that chair go as she ended up on the ground next to him.

CHRISTINA pulled up her beach buggy in front of Peter's driveway just as the sunset framed his house with an orange-red hue. Peter didn't seem in a hurry to get out.

She wasn't in a rush either. This had felt more like a perfect first date than their actual first date. But whatever else happened, sex wouldn't.

That's enough, Chris. Stop thinking about sex!

"Well, that was a boring day," she said.

"Uh-huh, very average." His tone was opposite to the wattage in his smile. Despite the sun going down, heat rose inside her.

"I think you invented a word," said Christina.

Peter's brow creased at the top of his nose.

"Wow-mazing," said Christina.

"I did not say wow-mazing."

She nodded and animatedly imitated Peter. "That was *wow-mazing!*"

"I'm sure I said, 'Wow, that was amazing'."

She shook her head, exaggeratedly mouthing "wow-mazing".

He conceded with a smile. "It was wow-mazing, all of it."

She nodded. Their faces were close again, their lips doing that magnet thing. Latin music swayed out of the speakers into a slower bachata track and the low volume only added to the sensual mood. She was determined to not step over any line. Not that she was sure where the line was anymore. Her thoughts had bounced back and forth like a sensitive tennis ball.

I wish he'd stop looking at me. Hell, I missed that stare — like I'm the only person on the planet. Look at those big bear eyes. I'm not going in. I can't.

"I'm glad you didn't stop your aging. You're even more beautiful now."

Velvet heat flowed through her. Teasing, torturous currents. She broke the magic by turning towards the house.

I swear even the house is winking at me to come in…

"Just how I remember it," she said.

They'd lived with his Mom till she died then he inherited the house. Peter ensured her gregarious garden was well looked after by professionals; Linda's green thumb hadn't survived to the next generation. The only change Christina could make out was the loft on top of the garage at the bottom of the long driveway.

"Come in, I'll show you my studio. You should see my new sub-woofer," Peter added the last sentence in his best baritone Barry White impersonation.

She was thrown back to a professional studio years ago. The rest of Peter's band had gone after recording a demo track. Peter was sitting on a pulsating speaker. When he invited her to join him she didn't need a second invitation. The few beers they'd had, mixed with the sub-woofer rhythm, created an irresistible cocktail. One of her all-time favorite sensual moments. Whenever she watched a scene in a movie or TV of a couple having sex on a washing machine, she laughed. That's so blasé. She'd take the erotic beat of a sub-woofer anytime.

Look at that cheeky grin. There's no way she would go anywhere near his sub-woofer.

"Forget your studio. I want to see my baby!" She took off down the driveway and Peter chased after her.

She giggled as they tried to squeeze through the side door of the garage at the same time. Then her giggles crashed in her throat when she saw Jane painting.

"Hello Peter," said JANE, who was as startled and disappointed as they were, thrown out of her primary colors and deep into primal feelings.

She'd heard them teasing and sniping as they ran down the driveway, so had a tiny bit of time to prepare. But a hundred hours' notice wouldn't have been enough to quell the instant tension and disappointment swelling inside her.

Yet again, Jane cursed the heightened emotions Up Here. It was much easier to ignore her feelings, or at least suppress them, in normal life. Irony or hypocrisy, considering she had made her career out of unwrapping other people's inner-worlds.

She had thought it would be a nice surprise for Peter to see her painting for the first time Up Here, in the very place he proposed. She was also looking forward to making love for the first time since… but the impact of Peter and Christina giggling their way into the garage dried her creative juices, crushed her libido and crashed her heart onto the concrete floor.

"Hell… hello," mumbled Peter.

"Jane," said Christina.

Christina's cold formality froze Peter in the doorway. Christina marched next to her Mustang, back straight, chin high, shoulders wide.

"Hello, Christina." Jane strived for natural, friendly and it came out like a wicked witch. She struggled to center herself.

Peter's eyes darted between her and Christina, like he was struggling to reconcile what was happening with the two soul sisters he remembered. What a mess.

He shuffled forward and pecked her on the cheek. "Looks good," he said, pointing at her painting.

"It's horrible, I feel like a beginner again."

She kept one eye on Christina as she checked out the garage. Christina pointed to the corner bench, once her work bench, now filled with Jane's brushes, palettes and paint containers.

"What happened to my old tools?"

Empty nails and hooks spotted the wall where tool shapes were marked out.

"Jane donated them to your old school."

Peter almost ducked as Christina swung around to throw a piercing laser beam glare directly at her. She'd never seen her so ferocious; no, that's not true. She'd never been the recipient of Christina's anger. Hate. Venom.

"Old tools, old school." Peter tried to lighten the moment

with a silly voice and flimsy defense. Bless him, but he didn't have a chance.

"Nothing abstract about your work," said Christina. She patted the tarp-covered car. "At least you didn't throw her out."

Jane put her brush down as Christina moved to the front of her Mustang and gently began removing the tarp. Then, in one big swing, she flipped the whole cover off, filling the garage with a cloud of thick dust.

Jane tried to cover her canvas from the dust, but it was pointless. The wet oil paint provided a sticky soft landing for the floating particles.

"Classic passive-aggressive," she said.

Peter winced, but Christina ignored the barb. She turned to Peter and pointed at her Mustang. "I'll pick this up tomorrow."

"Sure. Yeah. Anytime."

Christina walked to the door, looked at Jane, then at Peter. She looked like she might be tearing up.

"Drive safe, Chris." Peter's words sounded lame and desperate as they hobbled after Christina.

But they hurt. Seeing Peter so concerned about Christina hurt. The tiny chink of shame in her brain was buried by a fierce uncontrollable pain in her core.

CHRISTINA heard Peter's words only as sounds under the sledgehammer beat pounding in her heart.

How many times did Peter and Jane have *fun* in that garage right next to her baby?

She wrenched herself back to the moment; there was enough real torture without her imagination adding to it. She dived into her buggy and started it before she was even sitting straight then squealed the tires as fast and far as she could get from Peter's house.

Which was about one hundred yards.

She pulled over just as the pain exploded out of her body, pain surfing waves of tears. She collapsed over the steering wheel, head on her shaking hands, dragged back to the horrible early months after her death. The fierce aching for Peter that had so often left her curled up on the floor, crumpled by the intensified emotions Up Here. If it wasn't for Linda miraculously turning up each time to nurture her slowly back to some normality, she might still be on her bedroom floor nine years later.

They may have been base jumping earlier but it wasn't till she saw Jane with Peter in his garage that she hit rock bottom.

Christina's guitar-riff ringtone blared through her handbag. She let it ring out, still crying.

The guitar riff blared again.

She rummaged through her bag and stared at the screen for a moment before answering.

"So, how was the date, Christinarella?" said Linda.

Christina howled.

"Oh petal, what happened?"

"J-Jane happened. She was in the garage."

"Where are you? I'll be right there."

"No, not here." She gripped the steering wheel hard. "Your place in ten."

She took three slow breaths and got her pathetic sobbing under control.

"OK. Drive safe, Chris."

"Drive safe, Chris."

Pain ripped through her. She hit end on the phone, clutched her stomach and surrendered to her cries.

Pictures

PETER couldn't have missed the anger in Christina's voice, the pain in her eyes, or the hint of tears. He ran to the garage door but couldn't follow her; an emotional bungee rope reminded him of Jane. He just stood there, one foot in the garage, one out.

The first time the three of them were in the same space was always going to be a delicate walk along a sensitive tightrope in gale force winds. He hadn't been in any hurry for that catch-up. Plus, he had hoped for the seminal moment to be a more planned event.

Delusional.

The way things panned out in the icy garage, no level of planning would have made a difference.

When he stepped back in he was relieved to see Jane packing up. It gave them both a moment to avoid eye contact and talking about what just happened. And avoid trying to understand how he felt. He couldn't believe his time with

Christina had to end on another low; he felt badly for both Christina and Jane.

The only clear picture that rose above the emotional dust in the garage was the obvious tension which existed between Jane and Christina. He'd never seen them argue, let alone be angry with each other. The gulf between them now was undeniable. The cold pain that swirled inside him was powered by a current of guilt. He'd become the iceberg wedged between their tropical friendship.

"Looks like the two of you had a fun time," said Jane, without looking up.

"It was OK." He didn't feel comfortable diluting the fun with Christina, but saw no point adding fuel to Jane's singeing tone.

"When are you painting again?"

"Not sure."

He moved close to Jane. "You don't need to be jealous." He winced as soon as the words came out; it was like telling someone who was panicking not to panic.

Jane loaded and fired her glare. Both barrels.

"Sorry, I didn't mean to—"

"Jealousy isn't part of my DNA."

He had no compass for the jungle of tension they'd been dumped in, no landmark in their relationship that he could rely on to lead them out.

"What is our DNA now?" It was a question to himself that slipped out.

Jane faced him. "Good question. I don't know the answer. I do know you and Christina looked a lot more than just OK."

He stepped in front of her before she reached the door.

"You insisted I see her."

"I'm glad it's working out."

"Now who's being passive-aggressive?"

"I'm not." She scrunched up the canvas she'd been working on and dumped it in the bin.

"You promised to take me to the movies tonight. I still want to go. With you." He stepped closer.

Jane closed her eyes and pulled down on her t-shirt, like she was anchoring herself. When she opened them, he was back in familiar territory, care and love back in her blue skies. Although, there was still a hint of confusion on her brow. She nodded.

He kissed her cheek.

Tap, tap.

They turned to see a sheepish Keith in the doorway. "Sorry, I didn't know whether to knock or head back. The doorbell wasn't answering and—"

"This is Keith," Peter said to Jane. He was pleased to see Keith; he could provide a clean buffer to the horrible few minutes they'd just slashed through.

"Yes, yes, I'm Keith. Hello…"

"Jane, this is Jane."

Keith looked at him, scratching his head. "I thought you were with…"

Call yourself a mentor, you just unraveled some great work here!

"He was," said Jane.

There was an awkward beat as Keith studied the tarp on the floor. Peter glared at Keith, jerking his head towards the door.

"Nice to meet you, Jane. I'll come back tomorrow Peter," said Keith.

"Yes, yes, tomorrow—"

"Don't be silly," said Jane. "We were just going to the movies. You should join us."

Peter tried to wave Keith out without Jane seeing him.

"No, no, I better go, I've got… plans."

Jane glanced at Peter and he dropped his arms, forcing a smile.

Jane stepped closer to Keith. "Please, Keith. I insist." She flashed her smile and Keith melted.

"Well, if you insist, how can I resist?"

"That's very poetic, Keith. We can compare notes on Peter's progress." Jane took Keith by the arm and led him out.

Peter thought about dropping to the floor and rolling himself up in the dusty tarp. His two cherished worlds had collided in that garage and the big bang was still reverberating inside his soul.

At least tonight will finish better with Jane than his last two dates with Christina. Even with a clumsy chaperone.

The first time PETER'S mom had brought him to the Astor Theatre was for Spielberg's *ET*. While she'd droned on about the sweeping beauty of the art-deco architecture, his imagination was in outer space. To his nine year-old eyes, the twisting ceiling sculptures were aliens reaching for the moon and the giant chandeliers spaceships.

In the foyer it still took time to adjust to the eclectic crowd Up Here. Folk in top hats, flowing gowns and long gloves mingled comfortably with guys in shorts and t-shirts and Goth girls. There was a kiosk, but also roving candy sellers in oversized striped chef hats pushing their trolleys.

Jane and Keith studied the movie listings, but Peter had already made up his mind. The setting and crowd inspired a joke.

"I see dead people." He stopped laughing when he realized Jane and Keith weren't. He was sure the *Sixth Sense* gag was hilarious, but apparently Jane had heard it at least 15 times in the last three months, mostly from her students. Keith lost count years ago.

Jane and Keith turned back to the giant movie posters.

BEING HERE Starring Peter Sellers, Written By Homer, Directed By Blake Edwards.

SOME LIKE IT HOTTER Starring Jack Lemmon, Marilyn Monroe & Tony Curtis, Written & Directed By Billy Wilder.

A NIGHT AT THE GLOBE Starring The Marx Brothers, Directed By William Shakespeare.

ARTHUR THREE Starring Dudley Moore, John Gielgud & Judy Garland, Written & Directed By Steve Gordon.

"It has to be Arthur," Peter said.

"Really, Peter? *Arthur*?" Jane said. "Check out the brilliant talent in the other films."

"This is the original *Arthur* team, except for Judy Garland. But she's Liza Minnelli's mom, which is a casting masterstroke."

On top of the acting talent, Peter felt the true genius in this film was writer and director Steve Gordon, who tragically died twelve months after the original *Arthur* was released. Peter finally had a chance to see a genuine follow-up to Gordon's work.

"Please, Jane. It will be fun… and isn't fun the best thing to have?"

"Mmm…" Jane's head was on that angle.

"You have a wonderful economy with words. I look forward to your next syllable with relish," said Keith.

Peter was impressed with Keith's decent impersonation of Sir John Gielgud as the posh butler in *Arthur*.

"Oh no, Keith. You're a fan too?" said Jane.

Keith nodded, blushing. "Many a time as a priest I wished to unleash a similar caustic wit. Alas, I neither had the lines, nor the inclination to ruffle the religious robes. So, I nurtured my inner-Hobson in fantasy only."

"OK, *Arthur* it is," Jane said.

Peter celebrated with a silly dance spin and bumped into a boy, about five years old, who'd been pretending he was an airplane. A choc-top in his hand acted as a missile, which hit Peter in the stomach. Some of the chocolate stuck to his black shirt, but all the ice cream ended up on the floor. The boy stared at the empty cone in his hand and his face scrunched up, about to cry.

Peter grabbed the cone and put it over his nose, then dropped to his knees. "You found my nose. Thank you so much. I can smell now!"

The boy laughed. His mother, carrying drinks and popcorn, scurried over.

"I'm so sorry," she said.

"No problem at all. This will wash off."

"Jason, this is what happens when you run around in a cinema without a co-pilot. Let's get you another missile."

"But look, Mom. I found his nose, I found his nose!"

As she led him away, Jason kept sneaking looks at Peter over his shoulder. Peter animatedly pointed to his cone nose.

Jason laughed every time. When Jason was out of sight Peter removed the cone. Keith returned with some paper napkins.

"His mom handled that well," said Peter.

"So did you," said Jane.

"I'll get the tickets and popcorn," said Keith.

Peter cleaned up his shirt. Still on his knees, he noticed Jane staring at him with a look he hadn't seen before; soft eyes, almost watery, her face glowing.

"What?" he said as he rose.

"Nothing."

"You like my improv?"

Jane nodded. "I've never seen you with kids before."

"Young or old, everyone likes to laugh, right?"

"Yes… maybe kids are your target audience."

"Coming from the Kids Guru, I think that's a compliment."

The intensity from her eyes ignited his heart like a hot air balloon.

"You missed a bit." She wiped some ice cream dribbling down his chin.

"Thanks. You missed a bit too. Some paint." He gently stroked the dry paint just under her ear. Then he stroked a couple of lines on either side of her cheek.

Jane kissed his palm. "Back in a minute."

He watched her sway towards the Ladies Room. Just before she reached the door she turned and smiled. He placed his kissed hand on his cheek and swooned with fluttering eyebrows. Jane laughed then disappeared into the Ladies Room.

Wow, that was a moment. He didn't know what it meant but he was floating with the warmth she'd ignited, glad he'd pushed for Jane to come to the movies.

"Peter!"

He whipped his hand down and turned to see Christina with Linda. His internal hot-air balloon plummeted. "Chris. Mom. What a surprise." He greeted them both with a hug and peck on the cheek.

"You're here on your own?" asked Linda.

"No, no. I'm with…" He hoped they could all get to their movie before Jane came back. He could always send Keith out for Jane after the coast was clear. On cue, Keith returned, juggling two large popcorns and three drinks.

"I'm with Keith. Keith, this is Christina," Peter said.

"Ah, you're Christina. Wonderful to meet you."

"You too."

Linda looked between him and Keith with Sherlock Holmes eyes. He could never lie to his mom and get away with it.

"Must be hard keeping up with all of Peter's women," said Linda.

Keith threw a sheepish look towards him. Peter took a tub of popcorn and two drinks off Keith.

"Thirsty?" Christina pointed at the drinks.

He nodded. "Yeah, it's been a long day."

Christina turned to Linda. "Maybe you were right about that destiny stuff. Looks like fate has come full circle quicker than Senna in a McLaren."

Peter waved a drink towards Linda. "This is my mom, Linda."

Linda put her hand out to shake. Keith juggled his popcorn under his left arm then took her hand nervously.

"It's a pleasure to meet you, Keith," said Linda.

"Yes, yes, I'm Keith. The pleasure is brutal — I mean mutual."

"That's just how I like it." Linda held onto Keith's hand and eyes.

He spilt a bit of popcorn.

"We better get going, Keith," Peter said.

He dragged Keith a couple of steps, had to get into the cinema before Christina saw Jane. It was a solution that grated more than lubricated his conscience but the last thing he needed was another garage scene.

"Well, well, well," said Jane, appearing. "Isn't this a cozy coincidence?" Nothing cozy about her tone.

She took one of the drinks off Peter. He escaped Jane's quizzical stare straight into Christina's deadly glare which stabbed deep into his stomach. He'd never lied to Chris.

Peter flicked his eyes to Keith for help, but Keith stared so intensely at his mom he was almost cross-eyed.

Linda stepped close to Christina. "Hello, Jane. Maybe this is a perfect little coincidence."

Jane leaned forward to kiss Linda on the cheek, but Linda extended her hand out. Jane took it. It was barely a shake.

He sensed his mom's tone and demeanor was at the opposite end of the spectrum to how Jane had described their day together.

One thing he did learn from his psychology degree was that when you're under pressure or stress, the last thing you learn is the first thing you forget. Obviously, his stubborn mom had reverted back to Christina's corner.

"What are you seeing, Pete? No, let me guess. *Arthur Three*," said Christina.

He couldn't help smiling when he remembered Arthur was one of Christina's favorites too. She'd watched the movie umpteen times at his place.

He nodded, avoiding Jane's eyes.

"Perfect. We can all sit together," said Linda, the person who introduced Peter to the classic rom-com.

"Together," he said; more surrender than agreement.

"Don't you love the surprises and twists at the pictures, Keith?" Linda grabbed Keith by the arm and led him to the cinema.

Keith looked over his shoulder, his eyes wide. When the couple in arms disappeared into the cinema, he could no longer avoid his precarious little triangle. Desperate to break the tension he opened his mouth, searching for a trusty gag, but the competing scowls on Jane's and Christina's faces scattered the humor from his brain, along with all the other positive words in his vocabulary.

He forced a smile and followed his mom's lead, holding his arms out for both women. Jane took one arm and bustled Peter towards the cinema in long strides. Christina scurried after them and grabbed his other arm.

As the opening credits rolled on screen, PETER smiled at Jane, then the other side to Christina, his ego tucked in the dark under his seat.

Before that day, he'd wondered a couple of times if he could share more than a movie with Jane and Christina. Had they been thrust into this situation because a three-way friendship and romance was the logical solution?

Based on the recent Arctic reactions between the three of them, the fleeting notion had been crushed by an iceberg of guilt. He became highly conscious of not favoring one or the other with any movement or accidental touch. He was a naked screen in the dark cinema, with two intense projectors focused on him from either side.

JANE'S brain raced in clinical overdrive, analyzing every word and action in the garage and cinema. How could such a sweet, warm moment following the choc-top nose turn into this? Her brain couldn't compete with her emotions Up Here. She couldn't sit on both sides of her inner consulting room. And "couldn't" had never been part of her vocabulary.

The door between her emotions and thoughts was initially jarred open by Peter. But back on Earth she could still count on her intellect for answers, or escape. Now the emotional door had been ripped off its hinges and there was no escaping the uncomfortable pain rippling inside her.

Intellect stuck its brave head up for a moment when she realized many psychologists and therapists would be out of work on Earth if emotions were this intensified. People would clearly know what their feelings were and not be able to suppress or ignore them.

But the ripple of pain turned into a wave that washed all thinking away. Jane was left with two crystal clear emotional pools: she loved Peter and hated not having him to herself.

Even though she was sitting next to him, CHRISTINA didn't feel like she was with Peter at this movie. It was the second time that day she'd sensed a chasm between them; the other being in Peter's garage.

Chasm. What an understatement. She couldn't remember ever feeling that way with him before.

Maybe it is fate after all… and a little payback. Jane mucked up my ending to a fun day with Pete, now I get to muck up Jane's date. And it's a pure accident. Linda's right, it's perfect.

But it was an imperfect pleasure, like bad coffee when you're desperate for a caffeine hit, the bitter aftertaste wasn't worth the super-short high. The rollercoaster of emotions with Peter that day left her inner-cup empty. She tried to lose herself in the movie, but even the loveable Dudley Moore couldn't stop her keeping one eye on Jane.

Linda squeezed her arm. She turned to see a grin on Linda's face that could have swallowed an aviary. Linda winked then reached for her drink, letting her hand brush Keith's. He jolted upright and squeezed himself as tight as he could to the other side of his seat. Linda had to cover her mouth to suppress a laugh. Keith's nervousness was so cute.

Cute on her left side, crushed on her right.

Tension had set up camp inside JANE and tension had never been a tourist she'd accommodated before. The short tram ride from the Astor and the ten-minute walk to her Carlton apartment seemed hours in the uncomfortable silence with Peter; even he wasn't his usual tactile self. The walk loosened her up a little and allowed more time to workshop potential scenarios from the night, explore options for moving forward.

One cinema moment seemed a positive beacon against a rocky shore. Her thoughts kept drifting back to it. She really felt something when Peter was playing with that boy; a bubbly craving that first surfaced when she thought she was pregnant.

"This is it," she said, pointing at the steps to the bluestone building.

"Nice... great location."

He wore the black t-shirt she bought him, the one with the three small ducks flying across his pecs. Her eyes slid down his chest to his super tight blue jeans. Her brain grappled with the right recipe for the delicate subject she wanted to raise while her body heated up an entirely different feast.

"I'm sorry tonight didn't turn out so well," said Peter.

"It's not your fault. No one's fault really. It's just a..."

"Crazy situation?"

Jane nodded. "You were really good with that boy tonight. You'd make a good dad." She took Peter's hands. She missed what he could do with those hands. Her gaze drifted up to his mouth, his lips weren't like the over-flushed mouths of male models in magazines or TV ads... but what a delicious delicacy.

"I didn't think you could have children Up Here."

"You can foster kids that die before their parents, just till their parents make it Up Here."

"Right... maybe when I grow up."

She kissed Peter. He didn't back away. Simmering honey oozed from his lips, sluicing through every part of her. She pulled back, their heavy breathing a private symphony in a cocoon. He opened his eyes and her inner-furnace spiked a thousand degrees. She could've taken him right there out in the open.

She put her foot on the first step. "Why don't you come up?"

Christina wrapped around her shins, the other holding her wine glass. "Seduce him just to spite me."

"She's going to drag him to bed," said CHRISTINA, one arm wrapped around her shins, the other holding her wine glass. "Seduce him just to spite me."

Linda lay on the couch with her legs curled. A mega box of Maltesers was between them. "Won't happen. I know Peter."

"I know Jane."

"Three."

Christina picked up three Maltesers and stuffed them into her mouth. Linda reckoned it was impossible to have negative thoughts when your mouth was stuffed with Maltesers. Always worked before. With the sensual texture of the melting outer-chocolate against the internal honeycomb, it was hard to think. Part of the trick was the noise from the mass crunching and how it clogged up her brain. She wasn't a melter; definitely a cruncher.

"Here it comes." If Linda leaned any more towards the TV, she would've fallen off the couch.

Christina sped up her crunching as Linda's favorite line in *Casablanca* got closer. Just as Rick's moment came, she hit the mute button on the remote.

"Of all the garages in all the houses in all the world, she had to steal mine," Christina said, mocking Humphrey Bogart with an extreme nasal whine.

"Five."

"Five?"

"Uh-huh, and give me the remote so I can rewind."

Christina threw her the remote, picked up five Maltesers and forced three into her mouth, then another, then the fifth. It was hard to get a Malteser or two into position to crunch.

Linda rewound the flick, then paused and pointed the remote at her. "Of all the pity joints and all the victims in all the world… seriously, Christina. If you keep wallowing like this, you don't deserve him," Linda said with a tone like a stockman's whip.

Christina stopped maneuvering Maltesers. Linda had never spoken to her like that.

"It's genuinely complicated, I get that but it's not over. Not unless you give up."

The melting chocolate and honeycomb was sensational. She closed her eyes to savor the combined flavors and melding of textures; she couldn't believe she'd deprived herself of this sweet melting pleasure. She savored every little trickle, then opened her eyes.

"You're right. There were lots of yellow and red flags today but Jane doesn't control the checkered flag." She straightened up and stretched her legs. "This pit stop is for fuel and new tires only."

"That's my girl," said Linda. "Now shush while Bogy tunes my engine."

The nuclear currents from Jane's kiss continued surging through PETER in every direction. He took in her tight black jeans and loose red blouse, red ankle boots and matching red lips.

Has she had that lipstick on all night?

Leading up to one of Jane's birthdays, he'd learned the brand was Lady Danger. Maria called it DMWM lipstick: Don't Mess With Me. He jokingly labelled it "Empowerment by Lippy", but only once. Whatever he called it, the picture of Jane was as dangerous as a box of matches in the hands of a pyromaniac, in the middle of Aussie bushland, in the driest summer. Incendiary. Irresistible. Insane.

Now she asks me?

His body flamed "YES!" with a pulsating power he'd never felt. He would have loved nothing more than to go to bed with Jane again, except…

Christina.

One way or another, Christina would be there in the morning, messing up the moral sheets. The nanosecond her name entered his mind, all primal desire shriveled up. He wasn't sure what the day's tumultuous adventure meant, other than their romantic triangle was more subtle and complex than he'd anticipated. Jumping into bed with either one wasn't an answer, just a deeper, major complication. He removed his hands from her waist.

"You know I'd like to… I was literally dying to. But I think I need some time on my own."

Jane's eyes and subtle facial movement gave away her surprise, her disappointment. It's the first time he'd ever rejected her. A dramatic reversal to their early courting days;

their whole history, actually. Ever since that first kiss, he was always hungry for her. He felt more alien now than in his early moments Up Here.

Jane nodded and put her hand on his. He hadn't realized he was kneading his left palm with his right thumb.

She stroked his left arm, from the elbow down. It wasn't helping his logical, moral resistance; she may as well have been stoking a fire directly in his navel. Jane ran a finger over his thumb, then over each finger until she stopped at his wedding ring.

From their wedding.

He felt the glow of her smile. Noticed her matching platinum band.

"I understand," she said. The care in her tone released his tension.

"It's not you, Jane, or anyone else. It's…"

"A crazy situation," Jane said.

She gave him a slow kiss on his left hand then on his wedding band. She turned then glided up the steps and inside.

PETER didn't know how long he walked after he left Jane. His best guess was all the stuff swirling around his head must have done about 2.3 million laps. Christina… Jane… his mom… babies… Heaven…

Dying was more complicated than he'd ever imagined. So much for "Rest in Peace".

He thought he'd dodged the father-bullet when he failed to dodge the car in Valencia. One of the benefits of everyone dying. He wasn't expecting this subject to come up after the garage and cinema tension between all of them.

The only thing that helped him jump off the spiral was the decision that he had to do something special, something original, to apologize to Christina. He hated lying to her about being at the cinema with Keith, rather than admitting he was with Jane, as well. As intense as their situation was, he was determined not to lie or mislead Christina or Jane.

He ended up at Sennasation. He scanned the deserted track for ideas, then smiled at the stack of old tires that had witnessed his reunion with Christina. He rolled a tire from the central stack over to the perimeter grass embankment. Then returned for another tire, and another. About an hour later, Peter sat down in front of the pit area and admired the tires laid out on the far embankment spelling "SORRY".

"Christina's going to love this. Job done."

The moment his words spilled out, his major dilemma flooded back in. Seeing Christina and Jane together in his garage today had bounced him out of the dreamy reunions he'd been enjoying. It was easy slotting back into a rhythm with each of them and what he'd expected with Jane, connecting again so soon after her death. A little surprising with Christina, considering the nine-year gap.

How does that work? Nine years, like it had been just nine hours.

His dilemma wasn't going to resolve itself. But he also couldn't force it. Hours of walking and hard labor with old tires hadn't sparked any wisdom. Mountain landscapes, painted canvases, car tarps and cinema screens... they all threw up one clear picture. The attention-seeking heightened sensations etched the image deep into his soul.

He was in love with both Jane and Christina.

Hell of a Dilemma

PETER smiled, lying on his back in the middle of the king-size bed. The full moon cut a swathe of light through the gap in the curtains, angling across his naked upper body.

Jane, in a black satin negligee, kissed his right arm and worked her way up to his right cheek. On the other side, Christina, wearing a sunset orange t-shirt and burgundy panties, kissed Peter's left arm as she worked her way up to his other cheek. As they both came in to kiss his mouth, they bumped heads and aggressively pushed each other off the bed. Jane jumped up and grabbed an arm of Peter's, pulling him towards her side. Christina quickly grabbed his other arm and pulled him back across the bed.

Peter screamed in pain but Christina and Jane refused to give in. Jane propped her right leg against the bed and leaned back with all her power. Christina used two legs on the bed, leaning back like a sailor fighting a yacht in gale-force seas. Peter begged them to stop, but they just pulled harder until

Jane and Christina pulled an arm each out of Peter's body and fell flat on their backs.

Blood squirted out of both shoulder sockets all over the sheets, walls and ceiling.

PETER jolted awake, screaming and flailing his arms. When he realized he still had his arms connected to his body and there was no blood, he stopped screaming.

It took a while for his breathing to settle. He hugged a pillow tight and stared at the phone, thinking of calling Keith. What was the point; the guy had no idea about relationships.

Who else could he talk to? He only had a couple of days left on his seven-day deadline to work out which woman is his eternal soulmate. But this wasn't a business decision; surely that was understood Up Here? Maybe Keith could get an extension.

"I feel like I'm cheating on both of them," said Peter.

"Alas, two souls I have in me," said Keith, as he poured Peter a glass of Shiraz and topped his own.

"Shakespeare?"

"Goethe."

"Never read his stuff."

"It's perfectly natural for you to spend time with both Christina and Jane."

"But it doesn't feel natural."

"It's natural to feel unnatural."

He picked up the half-empty wine bottle. "Is this your first bottle?"

Keith smiled, comfortable in his regal winged-back armchair. The lush green-brown pattern camouflaged his green jumper and brown corduroys. His silver hair — that never looked like it was combed or brushed by more than his fingers — combined with the large lamp beside his chair, gave him a saintly appearance. The coffee table was laid out with nibbles and red wine but Peter wasn't interested in food or drink. He was hungry for guidance and thirsty for a quick solution to his dilemma. His desperation in coming to Keith exacerbated his frustration; the only positive so far was Keith being up.

"Plato believes we all have another half, another soul that makes us whole," said Keith.

"I read his book. Maybe Plato is past his prime."

"Well, there is the rebel, Rousseau."

"Never heard of him."

Keith peered over his glass. "For a psychologist, you haven't read much."

"I got by."

True, he stumbled through his psychology degree only because it meant so much to his mom. Back then, he was always going to end up in music. "What's Rousseau's deal?" he asked.

"He believes we can connect deeply with a number of soulmates. That each relationship helps us walk closer with our own soul."

"Rousseau's cool. I'm proof. I fell in love with both, they both fell in love with me. They are best friends."

"With very individual souls."

"Souls? What about our hearts? I love both of them and I've fallen *in* love with both of them again, except now they're right here at the same time." He paced around in tiny loops.

The wall behind Keith featured dark timber shelves filled with books and records. Eva Cassidy's siren vocals floated from the turntable.

Seeking help from a man had never been his strong point. Glen was older and sometimes a wise counsel, but usually less mature than Peter; more of a mate than a father figure or mentor.

"If this is a parallel universe, maybe there's more than one. Maybe I can be with Jane in one universe and Chris in another?"

"Good question."

He stared at Keith, buoyed by the morsel of a positive solution.

"Good question, but same answer, I'm afraid. No matter how many universes, we only have one soul." Keith raised a lone finger to emphasize his point.

"I never would have picked you as an Eva Cassidy fan."

"Eva's big Up Here. Her gigs are sold out for the next thirty-seven years," said Keith.

"Really?" He shook his head. "I haven't gotten into the rhythm of this eternity thing."

"Not really a rhythm, more like one sustained note. It's up to you what music you build around it."

He picked up a Nina Simone album. "I never got into Eva, but Jane introduced me to Nina Simone."

"Did you know she was bipolar?"

"Jane isn't—"

"No, Nina Simone. With all those mood swings, loving someone like Nina would've been be like loving two different women at the same time." Keith emphasized his point by raising both hands, palms up, far apart. "That wouldn't be easy."

"You're not kidding. Choosing between Chris and Jane is Hell."

"Maybe you're approaching this the wrong way. It's not so much a choice, it's an internal search for the three of you."

"That was straight out of a self-help book. This is crazy. I'm stuck with you, a celibate ex-priest, and you've never even been with a woman."

"That's not fair."

"None of this is fair. Dying has turned my whole life upside down."

"Please sit down, Peter. Have some wine."

"That's not going to fix anything, is it? And what's with the stupid seven-day deadline? That just doesn't make sense in eternity."

"There is no seven-day deadline."

He stood in front of Keith. "You told me—"

"No, no, I told you *I'd* be with you for seven days. You jumped in and assumed a seven-day deadline to choose between them. You seemed to need a deadline, so I let you run with it."

"Let me run with it?" Even though his romantic dilemma had its own organic urgency and had to be sorted out quickly, Keith's words threw him back to the early years after his father left, when everyone treated him as a young child who should only be given crumbs of the truth. It simply fed his anger.

He headed for the door. "You're just like all the priests who were supposed to be helping Mom when my father ran off. All words and soft voice with no—"

"For Heaven's sake, Peter. Shut up!" Keith yelled.

He stopped at the door, shocked. It was one thing seeing Keith yell stuff at the murderball game, but this was personal.

Keith joined him, looking surprised by his inner-warrior outburst. "At some stage you need to find peace with your father."

"I need to find a lawyer and fight this one soulmate rule."

"There aren't any lawyers."

"Really? We have to represent ourselves in court?"

"No courts. Occasional differences are settled by a Truth Facilitator."

"Truth Facilitator?"

"There isn't any crime Up Here, but human souls are human souls, so there are still the occasional misunderstandings or matters that need an objective and wiser eye," said Keith.

"OK, let's do it. Let's see a Truth Facilitator."

It was stupid being angry at Keith; the dude didn't make the archaic rules. He put a hand on Keith's shoulder then headed out.

"You can't force connections. Friendships happen or they don't," said Linda.

The busy community garden must have stretched for an acre, attracting a cross-section of ages and eras; some planting or pruning, others weeding or watering. Refreshments scattered around on wooden tables and picnic blankets.

PETER couldn't see his mom's eyes. On her knees, she loosened up soil in the pot around a little shrub.

"I'm glad you were here for Chris. I get how you two have become closer Up Here, but that doesn't mean you should use it against Jane… or me."

"Pass me the rabbit."

"Rabbit?"

"The mini spade." She pointed with her soiled hand.

He passed her the rabbit spade. "Jane might be the closest I've ever met to a superwoman, but she has feelings."

Linda stared at him, holding the spade one-handed like a spear. "She's not a superwoman." She dug into the soft ground, eyes focused on the fresh hole.

He wasn't enjoying sticking up for Jane when it meant confronting his mom, no matter how stubborn but he hated the way she made him feel a traitor to Christina every time he said something positive about Jane.

"Every time you hurt her, you hurt me. Push Jane away, you push me away."

Linda put the spade down, the dark moist hole between them. "I'm not doing anything to hurt her."

He stared at his mom, hoping she'd take the silence as an opportunity to be more realistic.

"Hello, sweet Linda," called a voice with a country twang.

They both turned to see a friendly smile on top of a lanky body behind a wheelbarrow full of rich soil. He looked ninety-plus and his whole demeanor oozed friendliness.

"Hi, Carl. This is my son, Peter."

"So, this is the strapping young man you've been telling us all about." He struck out his long arm.

"Nice to meet you, Carl." They shook hands, garden glove to garden glove.

"Pleasure's mine, son. How's your sweet Christina?" Carl winked at him.

He let go of Carl's hand and glared at his mom. Linda glared at Carl, her face on that angle. Carl's smile vanished, the fear in his eyes suggested he'd never seen that look before.

He turned up to the sky. "I better get on with my bit before the clouds get angry, hey?" He lifted his wheelbarrow and scurried off.

Peter sat back on his heels, seeing the positive: Carl had dug Linda into a deeper hole so she would finally have to back down.

"The honorable thing would be for Jane to step back. I just don't believe she can replace Christina for you," she said with a spiky tone, while her fingers jabbed at the soil.

"And you can't replace Jane for Christina. They were friends for twenty years before you met Christina." He dug the line in hard with a full-sized verbal spade.

He rubbed his thighs with the gardening gloves, leaving brown-black streaks on the denim. The confusion in her eyes confirmed she'd never considered the Christina-Jane friendship angle, her small role in keeping two soul sisters apart.

"This," he said, placing his gloved right hand over his heart, "isn't a community garden, Mom. You don't get to choose which plants go where."

She stuck her hands in to remove the plant from the pot then stopped and faced him. "I'm sorry, you're right. I'm the one who needs to step back."

Tension streamed out of him.

"What did you say these things are?" he said, pointing to the plant beside Linda.

"Burgundy Nandina."

"I like the red and green leaf combo."

"Sprouts pretty white flowers in spring too."

"Come on, let's get this thing in before the clouds get angry, hey?"

She grinned at his impersonation of Carl then placed the plant in the hole she'd prepared.

He helped her fill the hole with soil using their hands.

PETER and Keith were perched in curved seats that hung by a thick rope. The seats were at opposite ends of a huge set of Scales of Justice. The timber t-frame took up a large part of the vast room. His frustration with Keith's lack of worthwhile guidance wasn't helped by this strange see-saw type scale that required them to use a short step ladder just to sit down; their feet dangled a meter above the floor. They had to be weighed on normal scales first so that the unit could ensure they were in perfect balance. Every time he fidgeted, they both bobbled.

"Is this really necessary? I don't feel comfortable," said Peter.

"Just relax and—"

"If I need another quote from a self-help brochure, I'll ask for it." His attack and twist towards Keith made his seat spin one hundred and eighty degrees, back and forth. "This contraption is a joke." He was close to jumping off and leaving.

The room was a blend between the workspace of a psychoanalyst and a lawyer, but with much higher ceilings to fit the human scale of justice. There were floor to ceiling shelves crammed with books, large volumes and binders. A wide computer screen looked out of place to the side of the wide mahogany desk.

On the way there, Keith had explained that Truth Facilitators were selected from a wide range of the community. Legal training was the least important quality; common sense and a sense of fairness that came with wisdom were the key factors.

This Truth Facilitator happened to be Sigmund Freud. Apparently he had taken to the cultural soul of Melbourne. It reminded him of his beloved Vienna, only warmer and with better coffee. He certainly looked like the photos Peter had seen: bespectacled tight eyes, short silver beard, long sloping forehead and that piercing stare which questioned your every move.

Freud's head popped up from behind his desk. He was on his knees beside his big leather chair. "Tell me, is one of these women your mother?"

"No!" He and Keith blurted simultaneously.

Freud squinted at each of them as they bobbed up and down. "That's part of the magic in the justice seat scales. Unless your two souls are in balance, no one is comfortable."

"How can anyone be comfortable in this thing? Is it really necessary?" he said.

"I didn't mean your actual mother. Maybe one is more like your mother?"

"Well that's an interesting obser—" Keith began.

"Saint Virgin here is suddenly an expert on women and romance," Peter interrupted.

Freud studied him for a moment, opened his mouth to say something then closed it. Freud crawled around to the front of the desk, searching for something, his nose only inches from the plush carpet.

"I'm sure it's here somewhere… aha!" said Freud.

He picked up a paperclip and held it gently between his thumb and forefinger towards the light, like a jeweler admiring a rare gem. He bounced up and walked to a table featuring an object about three feet high, covered by a sheet. He unveiled a silver swan sculpted entirely from paperclips. Freud added the new paperclip delicately, then flicked on a switch. Five mini spotlights threw a variety of colors onto the sculpture from different angles.

"It takes every piece to…" Freud trailed off, entranced by his glinting swan.

Keith glanced at Peter like he was also questioning the sanity of Freud and whether they were wasting their time.

"This is madness. I'm going," said Peter.

Freud snapped out of his trance. "Ah, yes. Two soulmates."

Peter tried to settle back in his seat. His movement made him and Keith swing back and forth.

Freud searched his bookshelves and picked out a huge, leather-clad volume then plonked it on his desk, stirring up a cloud of dust. He slowly flipped through the pages.

"Uh-huh, I remember this now. Two soulmates is possible."

"For a transition consultant, you haven't read much, have you?" Peter said to Keith. To Freud, he added, "Thank you.

You've made my day."

"I said possible."

"What do you mean possible? Can I or can't I?"

"That can only be judged by members of our community."

"Like a jury?" said Peter.

Freud nodded as he studied Peter and Keith settling on the scales.

"How many people?" asked Keith.

"Two."

"Just two? That just doesn't make sense. Two is a small sample, plus it's an even number. Do you have the casting vote in a one-all deadlock?"

Freud shook his head as his eyes glowed above a rare grin. "It's so logical, it's brilliant. The only two people who may determine whether you can have two soulmates are…" Freud sat back and polished his spectacles.

Peter and Keith finally found balance on the scales.

Freud replaced his spectacles then leaned forward, aiming his piercing stare at Peter. "Christina and Jane."

Peter spun his head towards Keith. "You brought me here to hear this?" His agitation threw the scales off balance again.

"There is another thing. Watching you today… it suggests you have a problem with authority," said Freud.

"You didn't question anything in your first week?"

Freud ignored Peter's question. "Tell me about your father."

He jumped off his seat which made Keith slam to the floor.

"If you people could just focus. This has nothing to do with my father. I have a heart that's torn in two. That's all. Simple."

Peter stormed out, slammed the door behind him.

Outside, the fresh air gave PETER a fresh perspective. Actually, it was more his old perspective. He decided to go back to Plan A: spend more time with both Christina and Jane. Although originally it wasn't a plan, it was just the natural thing he fell into. No more clumsy ex-priests or out-of-date facilitators with ridiculous fancy playground seats. He would just hang out with both women.

I have to ride through this head on. Be brave.

They were all smart, mature adults. Any conflict or awkward moments would only help peel back the layers covering the answer. At the very base of his dilemma, the common ground in their triangle was love.

Surely only good could come from genuine love?

Hell

CHRISTINA glimpsed Peter approaching out of the corner of her eye, determined to fight her inner-warmth. It wasn't easy.

Since the garage and cinema fiasco, her world had been fishtailing all over the place. Working on her baby was the perfect escape. It always was.

"Hey," said Peter.

"Hey," she said, head buried under the raised Mustang bonnet.

"Did you like my apology? Took me ages to spell 'sorry' with the tires. After I walked Jane home—"

She jerked her head up. *Does he really have no idea how his words bounce around my heart like a dodgem car? Crash! Smash! Bash! Linda would've ordered me to shove a dozen Maltesers in my mouth.*

There must have been some fierce look on her face because Peter took a half-step back. "After I walked Jane to her apartment building, I came straight here to surprise you."

She felt foolish and flushed with an oozy happiness at the same time. He didn't sleep with her. She dived back under her bonnet before her face gave her away with a stupid smile or something.

"And it took us ages to re-stack them," she said. She pushed up her bandana with the back of her hand, moving hair out of her eyes.

"Oh, sorry."

She didn't mean to crush his energy but didn't know how to be with him now.

"Chris, I really am sorry I lied to you at the cinema. I was trying to avoid hurting you and I made it worse. I'm sorry."

She never could resist that tone in his voice, it flowed through her like caramel-centered chocolate. She straightened up and saw the care in those crazy-big eyes.

"I know, Peter. It's OK."

Peter smiled then pointed at her cheek, "Grease marks."

"Maybe it's war paint."

He brushed the back of his fingers over them. "More like birthmarks, these days," he said.

She liked that. His touch and the idea that she was kind of reborn Up Here with grease marks on her face.

"I love your persistence with this thing. Do you remember how many times it broke down on us?" he said.

Working on her Mustang couldn't be an escape from Peter if he kept shooting them back to fun memories they had with the car. To redirect the conversation, she decided to share some of what she'd learnt through her early days of therapy Up Here.

"I think it used to break down because I worked on it with anger, mainly at my claustrophobic parents. I wasn't strong enough to go my own way. Now I work on this baby with love." She patted the engine. "It took me a while to sort out that stuff about my parents."

"This is like a conspiracy. You're the third person in twenty-four hours to suggest I have issues with my father!"

She studied Peter, surprised by his outburst and the tension in his face. "I was talking about me and my parents, Pete. I never mentioned your dad."

He looked down at her engine and around all the parts sitting on the edge of the car, workbench then her.

"I've got to go. Catch you soon?"

She nodded.

He pecked her on the lips. "Mystery o'clock?"

She smiled as he ran out of the workshop, "Sure, mystery o'clock," she shouted. The back of her hand floated up to her mouth, holding in the warmth of his lips.

"Some establishments you walk into and you know the proprietors are in their element. The magic touch. It's impossible to walk into *Linda's Love 'N Lace* without feeling sensual and romantic. Linda has stocked her pride and joy with lingerie and other accessories that are elegant, eye-catching and original. The clever lighting and display throughout the boutique store creates an atmosphere both classy and deliciously cheeky."

PETER found it hard to align the magazine review taped to the front door with his mom and her shop. Another one for his "weird" list. It got weirder when his mom asked him to help out.

Linda created a new window display with mannequins while he held some of the lingerie for her. Most men probably wouldn't be comfortable in there. As the son of the proprietor, he certainly wasn't. But his mission was on a new bus and his mom was the obvious first stop.

"I get it now, Mom. All these years I repressed my anger about him." He had buried his father in a deep psychological tomb, layered with memory-resistant concrete and protective steel mesh.

Linda flittered on her window display.

"He left us and that indirectly caused your cancer."

"We can't blame your father for my cancer."

"It couldn't have helped. All the cheating, then the money hassles."

Her lips clenched, slightest movement in her jaw. He knew it was a tough topic for her, that's why he had to drive the idea. "I know what I have to do, Mom. I'm going to find him and get an apology for you… for us."

"Peter, you're way off track. Don't waste time or emotional energy on this."

"Glen always said wherever there's a front door, there's a back door. If there's a Heaven, there must be a Hell."

Linda shot him a seismic stare.

"What?"

"I've forgiven your dad."

"Really? In person?"

"In here." Spread her hand across her heart. "And you need to find a way past this. I can recommend a therapist."

"Therapist? I'm a qualified psychologist."

"Get over your ego and just think about what I said."

He glared at the back of his mom's head as she worked on the window display.

"Pass me that pink piece," said Linda.

He picked up the frilly French knickers with the tips of his thumb and finger then passed them to her. He'd never been able to stay angry at his mom for long and this wasn't the time to start. Sometimes you can't smash through something, so you have to go around it or under it; the message was ingrained from her reading his favorite book to him again and again as a kid.

"You know, Mom, of all the things you may have been doing Up Here, this isn't one I would have guessed."

"It was always my dream."

"Really? You always said following your dreams only ends up hurting others."

"Back then I was just angry at your dad. He was always on about following his dreams." Linda turned to him, raised her hands to her lips in a steeple, like she was going to pray. It wasn't just following his dreams that broke Linda's heart back then; it was the new twenty-eight year-old muse he took with him.

"He was the ultimate role model for selfish fathers."

"Peter, I was wrong. I was just projecting. You're the psychologist, you know what that means."

His eyes narrowed at Linda for a few seconds. Two direct hits from her doubled her usual quota. She turned and adjusted the mannequin. He shoved his fingers into his pockets and plonked onto the nearby stool, slouching against the wall.

"I've moved on now. Besides I knew exactly what I was getting into with your dad."

"Then why did you marry him?"

Linda stepped down, sucked in a long breath then released the air. "Because I was pregnant with you."

He straightened, hands on his knees. When he turned sixteen, they had made a pact to always be open on any subject, yet this piece of critical family history had never come up. "You hid this from me all these years?"

"How would it have helped?"

"I deserved to know… to know that not only did he not love me enough to hang around, he never really wanted me in the first place."

"He loved you, Peter, but he didn't know how to love you… or anyone."

"Except himself." He got up and stomped to the door.

"Please, Peter, don't walk away now. I need to—"

Ding-a-ling. Slam.

He took three heavy strides outside then turned back.

Ding-a-ling.

He sat on the stool, right hand kneading his left palm. "Sorry for slamming the door."

She waved it off, flipped the sign on the door to "Closed" then pulled up a chair opposite. "For all his faults and there were many, your dad married me the day after we found out. We weren't in love, but he knew how much I wanted a baby. He did an old-fashioned thing… the honorable thing."

He struggled to take in anything remotely positive about his dad after all the negative programming she'd dumped on him growing up.

"I was so desperate to have a baby I kind of forgot to take the pill. I hoped that would settle him down."

He stopped kneading his palm. "You loved him?"

She nodded and shook her head at the same time. "I'm not proud of the means, but it's impossible not to be proud of the result. I don't regret one second of being your mom. I couldn't imagine my life without you."

"Even with my ego?"

Linda smiled. "Even with your ego." She held his hands. "Are we OK?"

"No other secrets?"

Linda shook her head.

"We're OK, Mom."

The secret weight of forty-plus years unraveled her brow, floated off her shoulders, and somehow strengthened their bond. He enjoyed their silence while adjusting to the vital jigsaw piece of his life. After a while he pointed at the window display. "You're actually quite good at this."

"Thank you."

"Did you do a course?"

Linda shook her head. "No, once I trusted my instincts, it all came naturally. Did you think you were the only creative one in the family?"

He smiled, shook his head.

Linda stood back from the display area. "Sometimes you have to just sit with the blank space a while before you know what you want to fill it with."

"Another maternal lesson?"

"No more lessons from me." She closed the black curtain backing for the window display and stepped outside to check her work. After a few seconds she skipped back in and removed the mannequin's head. She pointed to a hat hanging high on a wall. "Can you please grab that pink feather?"

He stood on the stool, pulled out the feather from the hat and passed it to her.

Linda fiddled with the feather on the mannequin's wig then handed it to him. "Better idea." She stepped up behind the black curtain and placed the feather somewhere he couldn't see, maybe on the bra, maybe the hand. Linda shrieked with laughter and stepped down laughing.

"What's so funny?"

"Keith was walking past, and because of the curtain it must have looked like my head on the sexy mannequin and just bra, knickers and feather," she laughs. "You should've seen Keith's face, adorable."

"Keith? I need to talk to him. Bye, Mom." He gave Linda a peck on the cheek, passed her the mannequin head and bound out the door.

Walking through downtown, PETER'S frustration with Keith grew as he kept avoiding the question.

Keith had his hands stuffed deep into his pockets, shoulders slumped. "I've been failing you as a transition consultant."

"Just tell me, is there a Hell or not?"

Keith pointed up at the white building with Grecian columns featuring large letters etched into the wall: H.E.L.L.

"Very funny. Hell just happens to be a big building in the middle of the city?"

Keith opened the tall wooden door. "There's someone I'd like you to meet."

He squinted at Keith. The poor guy was trying and care oozed out of his pores.

"I really think this can help you."

Peter shrugged acceptance and entered H.E.L.L.

He surveyed the large foyer; a cross between ancient Greek architecture and exclusive club, including black leather lounges and a shiny marble floor. He read the words painted high on a wall: *House of Eternal Love Letters*. H.E.L.L.

He turned to head back out, but Keith grabbed his upper arm.

"Please trust me, Peter. If this doesn't help you, no more introductions or suggestions. I promise. You can even work with a different transition consultant."

Keith opened a large door held it for him. He walked through, immediately surprised and impressed by the enormous circular space. It had wide raised walkways around the white walls and a high domed ceiling letting in natural light. Keith pointed at the comfortable cubicles on the level below, all enclosed with transparent walls and domes on top. Individuals inside each cubicle were reading or writing from keyboards and screens, or pen and paper. Many of them crying.

"Some are writing letters or poems to people they left behind. Others are reading letters that were written for them," said Keith.

Some domes glowed in a blue color, others in blood red.

"What's with the colors?"

"They reflect your emotions. Blue represents sorrow, regrets and grief. Red signifies someone who has moved on and writing or reading from a more joyful, peaceful place."

One of the blue cubicles changed to red. The writer smiled through tears.

"That one changed" said Peter, pointing.

"That's the objective. Letting your writing and meditation help you find perspective and inner peace."

Peter was familiar with this concept, both as a psychologist and musician. Rather than a journal, the process of writing songs often gave him that inner peace. He still wasn't sure how any of this could help him but the energy in the building generated an inner-calm he hadn't enjoyed for a few days.

Keith led him into a large room filled with cushions, old-fashioned sofas and natural light from an atrium wall that curved into the ceiling. With his back to the atrium wall, a Monk meditated. Near the entrance, another man in a Grecian robe over blue jeans and brown sandals played table soccer, intense focus creating furrows deep on his brow, like mountain walking tracks. But when he noticed Keith, his smile released a thousand invitations across his golden-brown face.

"Ah, my friend has come to lose again?" he said before hugging Keith.

"No more humiliation for me," said Keith, waving at the table game. "I'd like you to meet Peter. He has some questions you might be able to help with. Peter, this is Plato. I'll be in the library near the entrance." Keith left.

He almost followed Keith out the door.

Seriously, Plato?

This guy didn't have a beard and cropped curly hair like most of the images floating around in his school history books. This Plato showed off long, dark wavy hair more like that Greek singer, Yanni. Naming their kid Plato seemed ridiculous… maybe it's his stage name.

Philosophers were probably rock gods Up Here.

Plato pointed to the other side of the table. "Please, honor me. I find it helps me reflect on life and death."

Peter hesitated then stepped up to the table. He spun the handles, impressed at the smooth set-up. He'd played a bit of *balakia*, as Christina's cousins called it, but he was better at pool. He wasn't there for any game; his mission was simple. This guy could either help him or not.

"Can you take me to the real Hell?"

Plato's dark brown eyes were deep entrancing tunnels; it wasn't like he was staring at them, more like Plato's eyes sucked him into a portal to another world.

"Feels like you are already there." Plato threw the ball into the game.

Before he could shift his players, Plato flicked a powerful shot forward and the ball slammed into the goal.

"I'm not very good at this."

Plato dipped his head a touch, keeping his eyes on the middle of the table.

There's something strange about this guy. Look at that silly grin and vacant stare. I'll wake him!

Peter rolled the ball in and attempted to smash a goal early by spinning his players as hard as he could, but Plato controlled the ball with his goalkeeper, seemingly intuitively, because his eyes stayed over the middle zone. Then Plato flicked it forward and scored again.

"If you want to find the path out of your hell—"

"I want to find the path to Hell!"

Plato leaned forward, dragging him even deeper into his tunnel. He waved his hand slowly between the goals at either end "The path is the same."

He'd seen shysters like this guy before; all eyes and charisma with a clever twist on words. "Whatever Keith is paying you, he should get his money back. I don't need a guy in a toga who runs a manipulative emotional disco telling me stuff I can read in a fortune cookie."

He walked out.

CHRISTINA suggested they meet there, desperate to find a way forward with Jane but no idea how to drive through the tricky terrain.

Monthly Chinese dinners were their tradition. When all the trendy foodies were migrating to Thai restaurants or modern "fusion-confusions", they'd stuck with vegie dumplings and Szechuan prawns. No matter what else was happening in their lives, these monthly dinner-dates were set in stone. She'd been looking forward to relaunching the tradition when Jane died, until Jane had dropped the three deadly words about her and Peter.

She'd settled on this new spot in Chinatown because of the joyful service of the maître de, Alex. She loved the Chinese proverb "Man who can't smile, shouldn't open shop". Alex was born to serve, with a smile your face instinctively tried to match.

She wasn't smiling. Neither was Jane, on the opposite side of the booth studying a mural of the Great Wall of China. The tension in her tummy battled for supremacy with the teasing aromas from nearby plates.

"You didn't even like him. You called him lazy," Christina said, with more spicy chilies than soothing tea.

"I liked him, but he was… well, he wasn't really working back then, was he?" said Jane.

"You never understood his music and how much blood he sweated for that band."

Jane picked up a menu but her eyes were too still to be reading.

"I would never have picked the two of you…"

Jane put the menu down. "That's the crazy thing. Our link was you. We both…"

Christina's heart went mushy and she almost raised her hand to squeeze Jane's. Almost. She shoved the sentiment deep under the table and stamped her foot on it.

"We both missed you so much. We couldn't stop talking about you. You brought us together, Christina."

"So it's my fault you fell in love with my husband?"

Jane glared at her. Christina didn't flinch, anchored her feet hard on the floor.

"You feel you deserve the higher ground here? Do you think if we knew *this* existed that Peter and I would have allowed it to happen?"

Christina didn't know what to think. She certainly didn't want to hear any intimate details about Jane with Peter. She didn't want to hate Jane, but now that Peter had created a Great Wall between them, she didn't know how to be with her. Not the way they used to be. And there was one nagging bullet she needed to fire.

"Before I died, did you and Peter ever—"

"No." Jane slammed the menu onto the table; chopsticks fell off the little bowl they were balanced on. "I can't believe you asked that."

Jane's eyes were fierce yet vulnerable with sadness and shock. Christina dropped her gaze to her little teacup and swirled it around slowly with both hands.

"Ready to order?" said a waitress.

Jane fiddled with the menu but didn't pick it up.

Christina had had a crush on Jane's brain from their days in primary school; like a crush on a movie star you know you'll never reach. But not even Jane's brain could pick a path through the messy menu their fate had flung them into.

"I won't be eating," said Christina to her tea.

"Give us a few more minutes, please," said Jane.

"Of course," said the waitress.

When PETER flew Plato's coup he ended up at his spiritual nest, his garage-loft studio.

In the whirlwind week since his arrival it seemed like he'd experienced a lifetime and in some ways he had. He caught up with his two dead wives and mother and the haunting ghost of his father. Glen was about the only significant piece missing. He'd been introduced to so many new realities and sensations it was impossible to find his own center.

Initially, the studio helped him cling to his musical dream. Then it became a silent monument to Christina, his original muse then his chapel for mourning Jane. The deep connection he felt in the space was just what he needed after the bizarre H.E.L.L. that Keith had duped him into.

He missed Glen, and the silly joker would miss him too. He could've done with his twisted wisdom. What would Glen have thought about Peter's dilemma with two wives being in the one space? Was he blindsided by an obvious answer Glen could point out? What would he have suggested?

Viagra.

Laughter bulldozed through his tense gut, railroaded through his tight chest, rocketed out his taut throat and exploded into the studio, testing the soundproofed walls and ceiling. It bounced back from the double-glazed balcony doors and washed over him like a spiritual cleansing. A baptism. A born-again Peter. Laughter dropped him to his knees; he leaned on the couch as his upper body shook. Tears streamed down his cheeks, happy, warm, soulful tears. It took a while for him to settle.

Saint Glen, you've done it again. You funny bastard.

He had another chuckle when he realized he was kneeling in a praying position. Instead of stained glass windows, Jane's painting of the lovebirds hung on the wall above him. He dragged himself onto the couch, slumped back and checked out the rest of his studio.

The wide mixing desk and two large computer screens in front of him, bongos and microphone stands on one side of the desk. His gaze settled on the two empty guitar stands sitting next to the balcony doors. One for his trusty acoustic Maton, one for his treasured Gibson Les Paul; both missing after he mangled them in his pre-death fury.

An ache deep inside sent a riff to his brain. He needed to replace them.

JANE struggled with the grieving pain, more intense than her torturous dying. She shut her eyes tight and pulled down on her blouse. She'd run this conversation in her head a thousand times. She couldn't control all the emotions but if she stuck to raw honesty it would show Christina their unique predicament was delicate, complicated and blameless.

She was determined to not let their thirty-three years of friendship float away into an eternal sea of oblivion. Their kind of connection was increasingly rare as families became more transient and suburbs turned into junctions, rather than communities. They had something precious.

There has to be a way. There has to.

She opened her eyes to see tears welling in Christina's. Her grieving morphed into deep care and pining.

"It's all right. I understand why you asked. I probably would have wondered the same thing if the roles were reversed."

"I don't know what's right anymore," said Christina. "This was a big mistake. It's all stuffed up now. Nothing's the same. It never will be right again." Christina grabbed her handbag and shuffled across the bench seat to leave.

"Six weeks around Italy on one scooter, that was right," said Jane.

Christina stopped. Jane's shoulders softened and she let go of the edge of the table she hadn't realized she was gripping. If she had to choose one gem as a highlight in a treasured friendship, those six weeks in Italy would have to be it. Who needed a whole gap year when you had a zany six weeks in Italy with your best friend?

"Pushing those sleazy Spanish guys off the gondola in Naples was right," she said.

Christina hugged her bag, a grin transforming her scrunched up face. What a crazy moment; one look from her to Christina when the two guys were getting too frisky and they'd pushed one each into the murky water. Hilarious. The gondolier didn't charge them because it was the funniest thing he'd ever seen.

"Letting those gorgeous Sudanese boys share our house for a semester, that was so right," she said.

Christina fiddled with a chopstick, grinning wide. Some stories you never tell your mom.

Christina didn't run, although she was still perched on the edge of the booth. Jane missed her so much and wanted her fiery friend back the way she used to be.

"Besides, you started it," she said, wiping her eyes with a tissue.

"What!" said Christina, wiping her eyes with the back of a hand.

"You stole Michael from me."

"We were just twelve," said Christina.

"Yes, but he was my twelve year-old."

"I only wanted him for his go-kart."

"I know. Michael didn't stand a chance."

Christina grinned, shook her head. Jane leaned back into the leather, grateful their banter was back to a Sharapova/Williams rally with more fun than grunt.

"Christina, we don't know what's going to happen… and that's scary. But this…" she held Christina's hands across the table, "this is as solid as the Great Wall of China."

"A wall doesn't sound like a great metaphor for friendship, Jane."

"It can be a wall, or a bridge we walk on. We've laid too many bricks in this great wall to destroy or ignore."

Christina's eyes widened, shifting her gaze up from their hands. "Perfect metaphor, Doctor Jane." It was said in a playful tone, the one she'd used in primary school when Christina first dubbed her "Doctor Jane".

Her tension disappeared and she felt a warm glow on her face. "Thank you, Christina Sennasation."

Christina's face lit up.

Alex arrived with impeccable timing, order book and pen poised just below his spotlight smile.

"Ready now?" Alex asked.

Christina studied her… then nodded. Jane squeezed Christina's hands, let go and picked up a menu. They were as ready as they'd ever be for whatever lay ahead. Their hearts and minds were, for the first time Up Here, in some kind of sync. Potentially losing Peter was unbearable. Losing Christina's friendship on top of that void… well, that was as close a definition of Hell as she could imagine.

Virgin Love

Gently Weeping Guitars. Great name.

PETER wasn't surprised his smile beamed back at him in the window reflection as he tried to take in the dozen guitars from the giant display. Two guitars in particular glimmered above all the other sirens, wooing him. A familiar Maton model and something he hadn't seen before, an electric Harrison.

A young woman inside the shop waved him in. She must have sensed which guitars he was drooling over and plucked them out of the display. He headed in.

He had no idea how long he'd been riffing on the Maton; he did know the rush, the pure exhilaration of playing. He was inside a guitar shop, but really, he was deep inside his Zen-zone.

The Guitar Guide, Katie, nodded with wide eyes.

"Awesome tone," said Peter.

"Yeah, man, these babies chose you," said Katie.

He put down the Maton and picked up the Harrison that Katie had plugged into an amplifier. Even though he'd never played this brand, the neck was a familiar neighborhood, the strings long-time friends. The instant he strummed his first chord, the sound and vibrations transported him again.

Two of the customers gravitated to him and started jamming, one playing bongo, the other a trumpet. They followed his lead and blended in seamlessly. Customers and other guides gathered around the impromptu show. Katie bopped her head to his rhythm, the store lights bouncing off her nose piercings and pink-blue hair creating a mini light show. After six or seven minutes the store was packed with people, everyone bopping, clapping, or swaying.

These musos were good. The bongo player had a rhythm and moves that matched her mischievous eyes. The trumpeter's horn licks transcended heights. They ended in sync, as if they'd been rehearsing for months. Cheering, whistles and applause exploded around the packed store. Body buzzing and impromptu collaborators grinning; that kind of musical connection didn't happen every day.

"These cats are Natalie and Erica," said Katie.

"I'm Peter." They shook hands, with that LA urban grip-and-shoulder touch.

"Smooth, man. Call me Nat."

"Bit rusty."

"Rusty as velvet," said Erica, waving her trumpet.

He was chuffed by the compliments because they were obviously pros.

"They're with the coolest band in the coolest town, The Nat Empire," said Katie.

Nat bumped fists with Katie.

"Too sweet, babe," said Erica.

"Nat Empire. Love the name, love your style," said Peter.

"You should join us for a longer jam," said Nat.

"Nah, I just wanted to feel a guitar again. Been a while."

"If you have the creative bug in your soul, it has to find a way out," said Erica.

"Yeah, kinda like a fart," said Katie.

They all looked at Katie, puzzled.

"Better out than in," said Katie.

Nat and Erica laughed.

He struggled with the attention, which was an unusual thing for him when it came to his music. He wasn't ready for any real performing, might just play at home a bit, maybe even start writing again. He never expected all this today. But, man; what a buzz.

"We rehearse Saturday arvo. The Spiegeltent, you can't miss it," said Nat.

"Wow, guys. I'm really honored… but I don't think so."

Katie jumped in with a little air guitar riff. "I'm doin' nothin' Saturday."

Erica played some air guitar to Peter as she and Nat moved on.

"Better out than in," said Nat, patting his shoulder.

Katie laughed loud.

Back at the studio, PETER tapped into his inner-rock child. He sat on the couch and hummed along with his new Maton…

posed with one leg up on the couch arm… danced with his new Harrison… fell to his knees Hendrix-style… did a crazy Angus Young impersonation spinning on his back… flipped up for a Chuck Berry duck walk…

The sweet euphoria of unrestricted private rock god-ing; finally, the heightened sensations were working for him.

He came out of his musical bliss and caught his reflection on one of the big computer screens on the mixing desk. He stared at the blank screen for a while then put down his Harrison, eased onto the leather executive chair and looked across the state-of-the-art toys. "I'm sorry I've ignored you guys for so long. I hope you can forgive me."

He was talking to the equipment, but the message resonated with his inner-muse. He flicked all the switches. As the green, red and orange LED lights turned on and the screens glowed, the whole room came alive.

"Look at that, you guys bear no grudges. OK, ready to make me sound better than I am?" He picked up his acoustic guitar then strummed and hummed, quickly slipping into his Zen-zone. A new melody wormed its way through his head. Every now and then he'd stop, scribble some words on a pad then play and hum again. It had been a long time since he'd felt a creative rush and he enjoyed every second. Recording that was easy. Lyrics, on the other hand, have never been his strength but he'd learnt over the years when he was inspired to just get something down. You can always finesse the words later.

The creative process continued to amaze him. When he slipped into his Zen-zone, he was allowed access to an invisible pipe connected to a sacred creative lagoon. Most of the time, especially his good stuff, he felt he was just a conduit, simply channeling what was already floating around in this lagoon. The closest he came to explaining the feeling was one night post-gig, tipsy on cider and Christina.

"It's like all gravity disappears. Physical gravity, problems, emotional stuff. You're not floating, just not touching anything. Your only connection is through this invisible creative tube," Peter had said.

A wide-eyed Christina had lapped up every word. "Sounds spiritual," she said.

"Yeah, I guess."

"That's your Zen-zone."

Christina had nailed it. *Writing and playing music is my Zen-zone.*

He hit record on the desk and played a new intro then hummed and strummed the new melody, but was shaken out of his Zen-zone when Keith bounded up the stairs.

"That-sounds-good-I-need-your-help," said Keith like a child who'd taken a swig straight out of the red cordial bottle.

"Now? Can you wait a couple of hours? I'm on a roll here."

"Could Napoleon wait for Cleopatra? Could James Dean wait for Lady Di? Joan Rivers for Robin Williams? Can love —?"

"Joan Rivers and Robin Williams are soulmates?"

Keith nodded. Peter wondered which other famous people turned out to be soulmates Up Here.

"Please, Peter. It's about… a woman. I need your advice."

"About a woman? Are you sure? Right now that's like the blind leading the blind."

"Yes, yes and love is blind, so that's perfect."

Urgent desperation spiked off Keith's eyes, coarse voice and messier than usual hair. His shirt was buttoned incorrectly, leaving a little more hanging on the left, a crumpled jacket in his hand.

"Did you run here?"

"Like a deer in the woods," said Keith.

More like a rabbit in a dog pound if a woman was involved.

"OK." He leaned his guitar on the desk, saved his work on the computer and shut it down.

PETER slapped his couch while laughing. "Juicy lunch! That's a classic. Ha ha ha!"

On his first ever date, both in life and death, Keith had crossed paths with a flirty, experienced woman. In a panic he'd spilt orange juice over her and bolted off shouting, "Lunch was juicy, thanks." Peter could just imagine the look on the poor woman's face.

"I could just go home and bang my head with a Bible," said Keith, on the other end of the couch.

"Sorry. OK, serious. Romance. What do you want to know?"

Keith studied his shoes, fingers tapping thighs.

"Keith to Cupid," Peter said.

Keith faced him. "How did you know when you were… when you were in love?"

He hugged a large burgundy cushion and drifted back to those precious times with Christina and Jane, warmth flooding through him. "It kind of sneaks up on you. Someone says her name and you catch your breath… or you constantly smile without realizing it," said Peter.

"That's exactly what I've been doing," Keith said, nodding.

He remembered the opening lines he wrote in a song for Christina, *Secret Conversations*: *"You just walk into my mind and confuse my concentration. That's OK, nothing's more exciting than our secret conversations."*

"And you can't stop thinking about her," Peter said. "Like you're having these secret conversations all the time."

"Yes, yes, all the time, like she's right there with me." Keith jumped up and paced around the room. "All the time."

"So, who is this virgin snatcher?"

Keith froze, hands holding his thighs like he was trying to stop himself from running away. "Can I use your bathroom please?"

PETER brought in a jug of water and two glasses while he'd waited for Keith. Waited for ages.

Keith resurfaced, tucking in his shirt.

"Are you OK?" said Peter.

"Yes. Thank you. Can't believe my shirt was all childlike. Embarrassing." He sat down.

"Don't worry about it. Women love that kind of thing."

"Really?"

"They find it endearing that we're human, that they affect us so much."

Keith nodded and sipped his water.

"So, how'd you meet?" Peter asked.

"I'd rather not say right now."

"What is this mystery woman like?"

"She's… she's a cross between Mother Teresa and Madonna."

"Madonna the singer?"

Keith nodded.

"Here's your first lesson, most women oscillate on the Mother Teresa to Madonna spectrum."

"So what should I do now? What are the rules of engagement?"

"There aren't any rules in romance. Most rules are anti-romance… they kind of help people justify why they should avoid relationships."

"That's scary. I struggled with the constrictions and contradictions of the church when I was a priest but since then I've struggled more without clear boundaries."

He passed Keith a glass of water. Keith guzzled it all.

"Do I stay cool for a few days, then send her flowers?" Keith asked.

"Maybe there's one rule: never use the word 'cool'."

"The highs and lows of emotional gravity are making me seasick."

"Emotional gravity…" Peter reached over for the pad and pen on the coffee table. "You might've missed your calling, Keith. Mother Teresa, Madonna, emotional gravity. You're a philosopher. Mind if I use those words in a song one day?"

"Really? I'd be honored."

He scribbled the words down then rested his chin on his thumbs, elbows on knees. The next step for Keith and his embryonic romance was important.

"I think this time you have to call her. Now."

"Now? I can't. I need time to get my thoughts together."

"You ran off in the middle of a date. Left her hanging. You have to apologize and be honest with her. Tell her how you feel."

"How I feel? I can't do that."

"Not that you're falling in love with her. Save that for when you're together. But you have to make it clear you like her."

Keith nodded as he stared at the lovebirds painting on the wall. Jane had captured a moment where one bird stroked the other's neck.

"Hey, lover-boy," he said, clicking his fingers.

Keith snapped out of his daydream and Peter offered the cordless phone. Keith stared at the phone like it was a poisonous snake.

"I freeze up every time I try and talk with her. It's like she knows the stupid button inside me and it turns on automatically whenever I'm with her or hear her voice."

"Wow, you really are smitten. Keith, love has that effect on all of us."

"Really? It's not just me?"

"Have you ever noticed how many times the word 'fool' appears in romantic songs and movies?"

Keith nodded, rocking his upper body back and forth.

"You have to step through the fear".

Keith stiffened, eyes wide as platters.

"I'll guide you," Peter said.

That settled Keith a little. He took the phone.

"I'll get the other handset from the bedroom."

"No!"

Peter froze, standing by the table.

"I'd be more comfortable if it was just the two of us on the phone," Keith said. "Keep it intimate."

"Fair enough." Peter retreated back to the couch and grabbed his big burgundy cushion. Keith moved across the room and sat at the opposite end of the dining table. He dialed. "Hello… um, hello."

Keith whipped his head up, eyes wide with fear. Peter nodded encouragement.

Keith raised the phone again. "Um…"

Peter encouraged him with hand gestures.

"Hello, yes, this is Keith." He listened and scrunched his face. "My run? Ah, yes, yes. I enjoyed my run, thank you."

He whispered to Keith, "No matter how far I run, I can't stop thinking about you."

Keith covered the handset and spoke to Peter. "That's very good. Do these lines just come to you? I'd never be able to think of something like that while I was talking to her".

He pointed to the phone and gestured for Keith to get on with it.

"No matter how far… I run… I can't stop thinking about you."

Peter gave his pillow an exaggerated hug, caressing the top with his cheek.

"You have?" Keith beamed a smile and whispered, "She's been thinking about me!"

He gave Keith a thumbs up and whispered, "Next time I'm going to spill my juice on you one drop at a time."

Keith hesitated, shaking his head. "Why would I do that?

If she's wearing a nice dress and I spill juice on her, it would probably stain. That doesn't sound helpful. You know, orange juice is acidic and can leave a nasty mess."

"Just trust me," said Peter. He grabbed his glass from the coffee table and gently spilled water on the cushion.

"Next time I'm going to spill my juice on you one drop at a time," said Keith into the phone.

Keith turned to Peter. "And then?"

"And then I'm going to taste every drop," whispered Peter.

He delicately licked and kissed the cushion.

"And then I'm going to taste every drop," said Keith into the phone. His cheeks turned crimson as he listened. "Not as delicious as your lips on mine," blurted Keith.

He gave Keith a double thumbs-up for his sexy improv and kissed the pillow passionately.

"You're making me blush too, Linda."

Peter stopped writhing with the cushion on the couch.

"Call you later, bye." Keith hung up.

"We just… that was my… my…?"

Keith nodded, delirious. "You were brilliant. That spilling the juice line was genius. I can't begin to—"

Peter threw the big burgundy Linda-cushion as far as he could and pointed to the door.

Keith bee-lined towards the cushion. "Do you mind if I take this?"

Peter waved at it. Keith smiled, picked up the cushion and hugged it gently. "I know you hate me now, but one day we're going to look back at this moment and laugh."

He threw another cushion at Keith and held up the glass of water as if he was going to throw it. Keith waltzed to the door cuddling the Linda-cushion, opened it and swung around about to say something else.

Peter poured the water over his head.

Dead End

Laying his soul on a public therapy couch.

No matter how many songs he'd written, whenever PETER played a new track to someone, fear and vulnerability lassoed a rope around his stomach, heart and throat. Any hint of a compliment and his ego would swing him into a Superman. Invincible. Flying. Soaring.

With one eye on Jane he strummed his acoustic guitar in the empty classroom. She placed three small colored objects on each desk preparing for the students. He knew Jane's brilliance at compartmentalizing, and at least she hadn't asked him to leave. That was a good sign, so he started singing.

"I lost my life and found my heart. You are an angel, you are an angel. I—"

"Just what we need around here, another angel song," said Jane, without looking up.

"It's just a work in progress. I've got some ideas for the verse." He kept strumming, kind of a holding pattern while he regrouped.

They both turned to the door when a bunch of kids barged through. A girl led a boy who was wailing and holding his forehead.

"Laura… Laura tried to… kill me," the boy blurted out in between breathy sobs.

"Nathan tried to take her bus and Laura just whacked him on the head with it. She may have been over the top but Nathan was a pushy little brat and deserved what he got," said the girl.

"Thanks for bringing him here, Stacey." Jane put her hands on Nathan's shoulders. "Where did this happen?"

"On my head," wailed Nathan.

Stacey pointed at the window. "In the playground. Get over it, Nathan. We know there's no pain."

"Nathan, you're probably a little shocked. We'll find a quiet place for a little rest. Then I'll talk to Laura." Jane held Nathan's hand as she led him out.

Peter watched Laura from the window. She played near the sandpit with what looked like a toy bus, pushing the bus along a track she'd made with stones and sticks. Alongside the track there was a large rock, about the size of three bowling balls. Each time Laura reached that spot, she sped up and crashed the bus into the rock.

"That's kind of how she died," said Stacey who'd joined him at the window. "School trip in the mountains. Some big storm made the bus crash."

"That's rough."

"Hasn't smiled since she's been here. Won't even play with me."

He squeezed Stacey's shoulder. "Time, give her time."

PETER sat down on a log near, but not too close to Laura. She ignored him.

He set the guitar on his thigh and strummed his latest melody. Sweet and light felt right. He'd read articles about the power of music therapy and Jane often talked about it. In fact, she's the one who sent him the links to the articles. He was always intrigued by the positive effect music had in so many cases.

Laura bumped her bus into the log, back and forth, harder and harder.

He stopped strumming. He could feel Laura's pain, her anger. He thought he was close to connecting but had no rational reason why or how he was going to achieve that, other than his first instinct of playing music. He caught the regular rhythm of Laura's banging and turned his guitar over. Each time Laura banged the log, he followed up with two slaps on the back of his guitar, creating a percussion riff. Laura sped up her banging, he kept up; Laura slowed down her banging, he matched her timing.

Laura looked up at him and smiled. It was the most glorious smile he'd ever seen. Dark brown eyes and sparkling white teeth radiated against her shiny dark-chocolate skin.

He stopped slapping his guitar, grabbed two sticks and offered them to Laura. She scrunched her face, eyes darting from the sticks in his outstretched hand to his eyes and back. She stood and took the sticks and banged them while stomping around the playground, with a natural Aboriginal rhythm, knees up, neck bending. He stomped behind her, banging his guitar in support of her riff. Laura became more animated with her arms, pointing the sticks to the sky, down at the ground, angled up, to the side. He joined in the fun dancing like a puppet, his inner-child pulling the strings.

Jane stepped out from behind some bushes where she must've been watching them, shaking her head in disbelief. Maybe a hint of pride too.

He waved her to join in. She shook her head, probably afraid to disrupt his connection with Laura. He persisted and on the next lap Jane joined them, picking up a rock and stick on the way. She slotted in behind Laura and slowly got into the groove, mimicking the girl's antics. Laura saw Jane and laughed, then made her dance moves zanier. Peter and Jane copied her and they all laughed at each other while banging away at their instruments.

Kids ran in from all angles, including Stacey, and created a conga line behind Laura; he and Jane happily drifting to the back. Laura snaked them out of the playground and through the school grounds.

JANE led Nathan, who had settled down, back in to the class. Laura walked towards them and Nathan cowered behind Jane. Laura offered the bus to Nathan. He hesitated but Jane encouraged him and he accepted the bus. Laura spun around and joined Stacey at the back of the class.

Jane placed her hands on her chest, afraid her heart would float out. In her work and readings, it never ceased to amaze her how much a child could achieve once emotional blockages were removed. They had the priceless ability to instantly move on. Somewhere along the line adults struggled with this natural gift. But that was a problem for other professionals.

For Jane, an only child, watching Laura interact with Nathan and Stacey filled her with a helium warmth she wasn't expecting. She had plenty of work to do back in her office, but instead she just sat near the back of the class, engrossed with Laura.

House music meets indigenous vibe.

PETER bobbed his head to the beat and fiddled with the mixing desk, arranging the sounds and riffs inspired from his "jam" with Laura. He'd gone a little overboard with electronic effects and needed to pare it back more to its rawness.

The percussion track pulsated around the studio mirroring the sensations zapping around his body. Sure, he'd dabbled in substances that lubricated the rock scene, but the temporary artificial highs couldn't match the buzz and ongoing satisfaction of creating music. He hadn't been this stimulated with music since before Christina's death. And it had never felt this good.

JANE had been watching Peter for a few minutes from the top of the stairs. She'd sensed Peter's focus and didn't want to interrupt. Plus she had a new perspective on his music. The piece Peter was working on was especially exciting because she witnessed the seed of the inspiration yesterday. Hearing what Peter had created from something as obscure as a pained girl banging a toy bus was impressive, even if she wouldn't be adding it to her own playlist.

Besides, Jane was there with bigger ideas to share and thankful for a few extra minutes to prepare. Her internal emotions on the way over had battled between joyous anticipation and potential rejection; unfamiliar territory. The music lifted her to an intoxicating inner orbit. It happened a lot since Peter turned up.

Peter sat back with his fingers interlocked behind his head, just listening, looking content. It was this lull or never.

"That sounds familiar," she said.

"Hey, how long have you been there?"

"Long enough to be impressed."

"Really? You like it?"

She nodded. "Bad time to drop in?"

"Perfect, just finished, at least for now. I need to let it breathe. I'll tinker with it later."

Peter raised the volume, jumped up and repeated the fun dancing they did with Laura. Jane laughed and joined in till Peter turned off the music. They hugged and sat down on the couch.

She forgot her mission for a moment under his adoring stare. She gave up fighting the domino effect his eyes triggered a long time ago. His gaze trickled down her body, like he was mentally capturing every essence of her. By the time his gaze came back up again, her body was warm honey.

"You've changed. You seem more… cruisy."

Other men had struggled to read her. Peter had always been able to see her just as her.

To feel that transparent to anyone was initially annoying, then scary. In the end, that's what attracted her to Peter. He didn't flinch. Most men she'd been with wanted to dominate the relationship, addicted to the power-play. Others were happy in a submissive role. Both extremes bored Jane. Peter found the inner-girl in her, whilst respecting her as an equal.

Her multi-colored dress, with splashes of blue that bounced off her eyes, wasn't short but had scrunched up above her knees. She patted it down.

"Love the big red buttons, they're like juicy strawberries."

The buttons were undone at the top, revealing cleavage but not excessive. She'd hung onto the DMWM lipstick, only because it worked with the buttons.

Warm honey and juicy strawberries… things could get messy.

She'd missed getting messy with Peter, but there were a few steps she needed to walk them through before she could roll around that sweet forest.

"You were inspiring yesterday," she said.

"Laura was inspiring."

Peter's eyes oozed love. She'd probably been a touch dismissive about his music before, before she'd found some common ground. She took her tablet out of her bag and showed Peter a video of Laura interacting with Stacey and Nathan, including lots of smiles and laughter.

"That's this morning. You broke through the little girl's heart and now she's coming alive."

"Wow. If it wasn't for her curly black hair, I would never have recognized this was the same girl."

"Music therapy seems so obvious now," she said with a tentative flick of her eyes between the tablet and Peter.

He nodded, staring at the screen.

"I really believe this is your thing, Peter. Your psychology training, your music… that combination is your gift." Jane put her tablet aside. "I spoke to Harpo. He'd like you to start immediately as the resident music therapist."

"You really think this is my gift?"

She nodded but strained to read his face, hoping he felt the same way.

"I'd never contemplated it as a career, but the way you just laid it out makes a lot of sense."

She'd never fallen out of love with the man in front of her and now she could see a path for them Up Here. Their own unique path.

"It must be a ball working with Harpo," said Peter.

"It's a ball working Up Here full stop. No bullies or megalomaniacs. Unlimited resources and all the focus is on the children."

"Breaking through with Laura was a buzz."

"Imagine doing that all the time."

Peter looked at his guitars in their stands then back at Jane. "So, if we're working together… we may as well—"

"I'm ready to move back in with you."

Peter smiled, then his eyes tightened a little. "I feel a 'but' coming."

"No 'but', just… 'and'," said Jane.

"And?"

"And… I'd like us to adopt Laura."

"You really did want a child, didn't you?"

She nodded, appreciating his sensitive, loving tone.

He admired the paused image of Laura on the tablet. "She's cute… with a hint of… you," said Peter.

"You mean, the banging a kid on the head with a metal bus bit?"

He nodded wildly, raised eyebrows, eyes wide. She slapped his arm. He caught her hand and she resisted for a moment, but her body ached to get past all this resistance, to just be the way they were before her illness. She kissed his palm and placed it on her right cheek then closed her eyes. Peter blew on her neck and it fluttered through her whole body.

"We miss the whole nappy thing. And no food thrown all over the kitchen," Peter whispered. His lips brushed below her ear, his hand caressed the back of her neck, under her hair.

Heat seared her soul. "It would only be until her parents make it Up Here… but that could be thirty to fifty years." Her words barely gurgled out.

"So, it's not forever." Peter kissed his way down her neck.

"Not that part."

"What about this part?"

She opened her eyes and pulled away slightly. She had one more surprise for Peter before they lost control. She held his hands and bent down on one knee then motioned with her head to the painting of the lovebirds.

Peter looked at the painting, then back. His glow confirmed he liked her reproducing his original proposal. Her tears made things blurry; she had to blink a couple of times.

He's nodding, that's a yes.

She hugged him tight then kissed him, relieved they had found their place in this new world. Sweet dizziness swamped her, lost in his lips, hands and tongue. She opened her eyes, looking forward to his gaze — the one he had when things got spicy between them — when his boyish face morphed into warrior mode; but something wasn't right.

"We have to tell Chris."

Jane had been so overcome with her dreams about Laura and Peter in the last twenty-four hours, she had managed to suppress Christina in deep recesses. But she knew better than anyone, Christina could never be buried in any recess.

"We should do it together."

Peter shook his head. "No, I have to tell her. It has to come from me."

"Sooner the better."

Peter nodded but stayed on the couch. Her lips ached for more of his. She moved in but they were stunned by the blaring of a ridiculous musical car horn.

PETER knew that sweet, silly car horn. He let go of Jane and stepped through the open French doors onto the balcony.

Christina and her sunrise smile, blending perfectly with her three-quarter red cargo pants and burnt-orange long t-shirt, stood next to her gleaming red Mustang.

"I've cracked it and made it all the way here! You deserve the first ride." She moved closer. "Get your bum down here, Mister Wow-Mazing."

Christina's excitement was infectious and he couldn't help matching her smile, flung back into the memories he'd shared with Christina and her beloved Mustang.

Jane joined him on the balcony and all smiles disappeared.

On the way to Peter's house, CHRISTINA'S inner-glow hummed like her Mustang's engine. Not one splutter from the beast that had driven them to more despair than destinations; a good omen. Her soul and machine flowed and so would the rest of their time Up Here.

He even died the same way, another sign. What are the odds we would both be run over?

It had been hard not to speed. Even though no one could get hurt, it was still frowned on; plus, she didn't want to scratch her baby. Not before taking Peter for a spin.

Now her head was spinning. Everything was spinning.

"Maybe you should come up, Chris. We have something to tell you," said Jane, with hands wrapped around Peter's arm.

Confusion and disappointment shot through her. "I don't need to hear the words." She looked down, struggling to find anything else to say. No fire, no pain. Not a giving in, or defeat. Numbness. Peter had made his decision and she had crashed the party.

"I'm happy for both of you," she said to the concrete, then spun towards her car.

JANE was surprised and embarrassed when Peter wrapped his arms around her waist and lifted her. Even though there was a beautiful symmetry to the instinct because this was the balcony where everything really started for them, when he courageously broke through with that beautiful heart, archaeologist museum line and she kissed him. It didn't feel right replicating the moment in front of Christina.

"Peter, this isn't the time to celebra—"

Peter threw her over the balcony rail.

She shrieked before landing on Christina, both of them splayed on the concrete.

⌑

CHRISTINA sprung to her feet, confused. As Jane scrambled up, she lunged and pushed her.

Jane stumbled, but didn't fall. Peter landed near them.

"You manipulative witch," she said.

"Me, manipulative? And you were going to take Peter for a Sunday drive to church?" said Jane.

"You won him again. Why jump on me?"

"I didn't jump," Jane said. "He threw me over."

"This is spooky. It's like the two lovebirds fighting in the cage… for me," Peter said.

Christina and Jane glared at Peter.

"Sorry, that was—"

"Enough with the sorrys, Peter." Christina was disappointed with herself for lashing out, but what did he expect? A good luck card? Then she registered Jane's words. *Peter threw me over.* The slightest waft of a hopeful breeze slipped through the tiniest crack in the floor of her heart. "So, why'd you throw her over?"

He looked at Jane.

"He probably didn't want to shout our news from the balcony," said Jane.

She felt Peter's hesitation. The hopeful breeze strengthened into a swirl. She wanted to hear the news.

No, she didn't.

Yes, she definitely wanted to hear it.

She needed to see Peter's eyes when he said it, no matter the consequences. He owed her that much. She mustered all her strength and locked eyes with Peter.

"So spill it," she said.

PETER was back to his natural state Up Here; totally and utterly confused. Just when his choices and his eternal future found clarity, a cheesy melodic car horn blasted him out of that ever-so-temporary comfort zone Jane had mapped out for them.

Peter tore his eyes from Christina to Jane. Gentle lines rippled her brow. He got a reprieve when a teenage boy chased a bouncing soccer ball halfway down the driveway.

"Sorry!" said the boy.

Peter raised his hand to acknowledge it was OK. A part of him wanted to start up a conversation with the kid, have a kick for a few hours. The kid dribbled the ball back up the driveway and turned out of sight.

"Peter and I are adopting a girl," blurted Jane.

Christina's face turned pale. She squinted at him but he couldn't face her, lowering his gaze.

The words had an edge no studio equipment or software could soften; his internal mixing desk lit up with red lights, there was something wrong with the track.

"We'd like you to be the godmother," said Jane.

He could see what she was doing. Even though it was a wonderful gesture, and he would have loved the idea under any reasonable circumstances, these were far from reasonable circumstances. Unusually bad timing from Jane; he felt for Christina.

"Adopting? You've never mentioned children before. Ever. Is this what you really want, Pete?" asked Christina.

He faced Christina, then Jane… then shook his head.

Jane stepped close to him and wrapped her hands around his arm. "Peter, I know this is hard, but you have to be…"

He motioned for Jane to stop, untangled himself, and moved a little so he could face both women. "I love you, Jane… and I love you, Chris."

"What we just said upstairs, that was real," said Jane.

"Yes, probably the most sense I've heard all week."

"Adopting a child is a big decision. I shouldn't have put you on the spot like that. Why don't you take some time to process it?"

"No, Jane. I was overwhelmed up there with positive feelings. I've never seen you so excited about my music. The whole Laura thing was amazing, but there's a much bigger elephant here."

"I might wear baggier clothes than her, but I'm no elephant," said Christina, crossing her arms.

He half-smiled at Christina's attempt at humor in the middle of such a delicate moment.

"The thought of being without either of you is driving me insane. I love both of you and I don't want to hurt either of you. Trouble is I can't be with both of you. And now I know I can't be with one of you."

The energy bubbling from the triangular volcano subsided. Getting the words out gave him some relief, but only relief by relativity; his heart and stomach weighed down by hardening lava that had nowhere to flow. By their dark, wax-like faces, Christina and Jane were suffering something similar.

Christina turned to Jane. "Maybe we have both been a little pushy."

Jane opened her mouth to retaliate when Peter stepped forward. "No one's done anything wrong here. It's just…"

"… a crazy situation," all three finished together. In a surreal moment, it was the first time the three of them had been in sync Up Here. Yet the bond that intertwined them, their deep love for each other, was not enough.

"It's a lot easier when there's someone to blame," said Jane.

Christina's eyes flared at Jane, about to defend herself. But then her whole body softened, eyes watery.

Jane kissed Peter's cheek, gentle and slow, then headed up the driveway. Her usual stride halved, the short, sudden goodbye no easier or less painful than the drawn out torture of her death.

"At least this time we get to say goodbye," said Christina, wiping tears with the back of her hand.

His own eyes filled with stinging tears, because yet again he was thrown back to her death.

"See ya, Pete."

"Bye, Chris."

She stepped in and hugged him tight. He wrapped around her as if one final hug would make up for all the grief and missing years and messy last couple of weeks.

She let go all at once, kept her face down and slid into her beloved Mustang. The engine roared and the tires squealed up the driveway almost running over Jane, who had to dive into the bushes.

Christina drove off to the left. Jane dusted herself down and disappeared in the opposite direction.

Energy drained out of him; he leaned back on the garage door and stared at two tracks of rubber fading down his driveway.

Who Are You?

I'm just in the way.

JANE longed to be sucked back up a tube. Out of the Arrival Lounge. Out of this so-called Heaven. Out of the triangle of love-torture. She slouched on the arrival booth wall, her hands on Ricky's young shoulders as he leaned forward with eyes on the tube and mattress.

All her life and early Up Here she was an enabler or facilitator. Helping kids, counselling Christina with her parents, guiding Peter.

How did I become an obstacle to both of them?

Falling in love with Peter was the huge missing theme in her life's thesis. More than that, his love became the glue that locked in every other chapter, creating the foundation for her heart to dream in unexpected dimensions. Like Laura. Now the thesis lay blank. All of it.

She'd volunteered to escort Ricky on his reunion with his father, Jim, because her real work was no match for the relentless aching for Peter since the…

Break up.

She clutched her chest as pain ripped through. She'd never imagined breaking up with him, nor had she experienced a relationship ending before that mattered. Peter, her romance archaeologist, was the only one who'd dug deep enough… and now she was buried in the ruins of their mutual discovery.

Jumping on him with the whole Laura thing was such an awful judgment call. As if she was struck with momentary alexithymia.

I should have waited. Left it till —

"Heeere's Wendy!"

Jane was jarred out of her melancholy by a woman who burst into the booth, wearing a t-shirt emblazoned with *"Naughty in My Nineties"*.

The Arrival Angel looked up from his tablet.

"Um… is this where Lina is popping out?" said Wendy.

The Arrival Angel smiled and pointed to the next booth.

"Whoops. Sorry." She rushed back out, revealing the back of the t-shirt: *"Why Change Now?"*

Jim rolled out of the tube and plonked on the mattress.

"Hey, Dad!" squealed Ricky, diving onto him.

They hugged, laughed and wrestled; nine year-old Ricky and may as well be nine year-old Dad.

Jane admired their connection through tears. Maybe this wasn't the best path to closure with Peter. Her heart and subconscious had invested in more parenting visions with him than she had realized. Her job was done with Ricky. Her own healing had barely begun.

She shuffled out of the booth but as she reached the end of the wall, a surge of pain rifled from her heart through her chest, all the way to her toes. Almost collapsing, she gripped the wall to steady herself.

"Heeere's Lina," came a shriek from the next booth.

Jane peeked through the curtain to see Lina spring off the mattress. Lina shrieked at seeing Wendy and they did an impromptu stomping dance before hugging. Soaking up this golden reunion of friends soothed her.

Why?

It took a few moments to acknowledge the instinctive reaction was triggered by her lifelong friend. Christina needed to be part of her healing, and she needed to be there for Christina. They had to find a way through this for each other. Whatever else happened they had to protect their friendship.

But how?

That was wow-mazing…

After another night where CHRISTINA'S bed had become more of a tormenting Peter-treadmill than place of rest, her first waking thought was his unique reaction to jumping off the cliff. She'd escaped to work, desperate for distraction as some hope of inching forward. Sennasation cannoned with noise as karts swooped around the track but her internal soundtrack still had Peter on high rotation. Helping twelve year-old Thomas with his seat belt, she was distracted by two women at the kiosk with their heads close, touching each other affectionately.

You should see my new sub-woofer…

She strapped Thomas's arms under the seatbelt, pulled it tight and noticed his hands couldn't reach the steering wheel but was focused on the romantic couple at the kiosk and pushed his kart off. She couldn't understand why Thomas's kart zigzagged down the track, turned into the middle grass area and crashed into a pole.

I can't be with both of you and now I know I can't be with one of you…

In the next kart Thomas's dad, Dean, was adjusting his helmet straps. Still watching the romantic couple, Christina banged the helmet down onto his head. Back-to-front. She pushed his kart off and it zigzagged all over the track, running through the middle and smashing into the stack of tires.

Peter's tires.

As Sennasation Crew Members ran to help Thomas and Dean, another Crew Member brought Christina her knapsack, gave her a hug and pointed to the door. She shuffled out, head down as she passed the two women kissing.

The greatest love of her life had been taken from her twice.

Standing on the mountain ledge where CHRISTINA last jumped off with Peter, there wasn't another soul in sight. She was absorbed by the lazy moon that seemed to be grinning at the morning sun. It brought momentary comfort with memories of the first song Peter wrote for her, *Just You, the Moon and Me.* Yes, there were some corny lines, but one amazing couplet branded her soul: "You make my body so alive, I can taste the moonlight."

What a beautiful thing to write for anyone. He wrote it for me.

Christina still struggled to believe she had inspired it.

I guess I won't be inspiring any more.

The pain flooded back and she tottered, dizzy. She leaned forward and collapsed over the cliff. No control or style this time; her body bumped and thumped off the cliff face on the way down like a sack of potatoes, ending in a contorted mess.

She slowly sat and scrunched back against a rock, wrapping arms tight around her shins. Not even for a second did the unbearable sadness leave her; not on the rough way down, nor the thudding landing.

A strong warm arm wrapped around her shoulders. For a moment she sparked up, thinking it might be Peter, but it was Linda. The irony destroyed her last sense of control; sobbing, sniffling, shaking. Linda wrapped her other arm around and held her tight. She smothered her head into Linda's shoulder, desperate to smother the raw, agonizing tears.

The moon, usually PETER'S constant source of wonderment and inspiration, had turned traitor: *"Just you, the moon and me. Three souls sailing the stars tonight. The secret's between us. Just you, the moon and me."*

When he wrote the song, the three souls were him, Christina and the moon. Maybe the song knew his future triangle of torture.

There won't be three souls sailing any stars tonight. We'll be drowning in misery.

Pain showed no sympathy, no sense of empathy, drilling between heart and brain, shoveling out any remote chance of apathy. As if apathy was ever an option. Arms pressed tight over his chest and stomach, he bent over on the crate, clenched his eyes tight. Other Vic Market visitors ignored him; he guessed they knew extreme emotional hell was the only thing he could possibly be suffering. Let him suffer in peace.

For a moment he thought he was hallucinating or dreaming, hearing the guitar of Carlos Santana. He lifted his head a touch and squinted towards the sound. The busker looked like his inspirational music teacher, Russ Zimmer, but as his eyes adjusted he could see they shared the same long wavy grey hair and good technique but that was all; playing a piece of haunting melancholy.

"I've got churros," said Keith.

"I've got nothing."

He twisted his head to see Keith waving an open paper bag under his nose. The familiar waft of warm dough, sugar and jam would normally have acted as a smelling salt, jolting him out of his deepest despair. But even his favorite soul food couldn't break through.

"You've been blessed with three amazing women, Peter."

"Three?"

"Don't forget your mom."

There were good reasons he'd ignored Keith's calls the last few days, or week, or however long it had been. "Please don't do that again. I'm suffering enough without reliving that image."

"You've had two great loves. There are millions of souls who would swap with you."

"They can have this now."

"You don't mean that."

"Yes, I bloody do."

"You'd swap all those great times with Christina and Jane? You'd rather not have had those beautiful moments?"

He wasn't ready for rhetorical wisdom.

Let me suffer in peace.

"Whenever the emotional pain overwhelms, just focus on a special memory with Christina or Jane."

Too obvious and easy. How could such crippling pain be overcome with psychology 101?

"You can't just think about the memory. You have to be there. Feel it," said Keith.

Despite his skepticism, he visualized Christina swaying to his music at one of his early gigs, the one of a kind rhythmic swaying that made his heart dance.

That eased the pain and he straightened up.

His mind drifted to the first time he and Jane made love. Slow dancing in her lounge room to Nina Simone, the sultry Joe Clausell remix of *Feeling Good*. Jane's teasing little black dress featured zips all the way down both sides and inspired another corny line: "I love this dress, one zip for you, one for me". He remembered her fireplace eyes… her hand guiding his to one of the zips…

"That actually worked," he said, taking a churro and devouring it in three quick bites. Keith watched him, bemused. He grabbed another churro and they munched in silence.

After a few minutes Keith bounced up. "Let's walk."

He stared at him. The intense emotional pain had subsided, but it left behind a cavernous hole. Maybe it was a permanent dark hollowness he'd have to get used to. The pain crept back in. Slow but unmistakable.

Keith must've seen something in his face; he waved the churro bag in front of him again.

A sea of junior soccer players swarmed over the Albert Park pitches. Parents clapped and encouraged them.

"It must have been hard for Dad," said PETER, arms wrapped tight around his knees. He dug his heel back and forth into the couch grass. The walk had been a good idea; it cleared his head enough to see all the debris swirling around his inner-world. Keith nodded, stretching his legs out.

Players calling for the ball, referee whistles and parents' voices, combined with the seagulls over the lake behind them created a cacophony of noise that sounded operatic by the time it reached him at the top of the grass mound. Next time he'd bring his digital recorder.

"When it came to the crunch. I couldn't do it," Peter said. "I wasn't ready to be a parent."

"It's not a small thing," said Keith.

"Yet he stayed with Mom… stayed long enough to make sure we'd be OK."

"He doesn't sound like a monster," said Keith.

"Then why isn't he here? Why is he in Hell?"

There was a huge roar as the blue team scored a goal.

Keith leaned closer. "There is no Hell. Not a physical hell. We all have a version of an internal hell; we all have our issues, our baggage and our demons. Some just have more. Up Here everyone has the opportunity to realign their soul."

"So are they in some kind of institution, like a prison?"

"No, no. More like a retreat while they go through therapy and meditation. They need time away with experienced 'angels'."

"How long?" asked Peter.

"For some, months, for others it can take many years. When your father's ready, he'll find you."

He hadn't realized how much the psychological stuff with his dad had been messing with the soundtrack of his life, until he recently cleaned up that inner-track. Keith's explanation only helped. He was comfortable with the idea that they would find their time to start a new relationship, with an eternity to make it work.

"So, Hell is just…"

"An archaic marketing tool," finished Keith.

"Wow, that's big coming from an ex-Catholic priest. Does that mean there's no God… or gods?"

Keith took a bit of time to formulate his answer. The breeze teased Peter with the delicious aromas from the nearby souvlaki stand. It had been a while since he'd enjoyed a souvy, as Christina called them.

"Try this," Keith said. "Whenever someone makes a statement about their god, replace the word 'god' with love. Does harming children come from love?"

"No," said Peter.

"Does blowing up innocent people come from love? Could someone based in love create natural disasters and diseases that kills so many people?"

He shook his head.

"Punishment and driving the fear of Hell is the antithesis of love, the extreme opposite of forgiveness and compassion. Sending people to a Hell says, 'We've given up on you'."

Keith's spiritual view wasn't clouded by stained glass; he'd never heard anyone explain it so simply.

"We don't do realignment and forgiveness well on Earth, do we?"

"It's easier to pigeonhole people as good or bad," said Keith. "Most people feel more comfortable with themselves if they can paint everyone else in black or white."

He nodded, accepting he was no angel when it came to this very human habit.

"But we all come in a myriad of colors, shades and texture. Sometimes we need a wise guide to help us realign." said Keith.

"Speaking of wise, I can't believe you took me to that H.E.L.L. house. What kind of shyster takes the stage name of Plato?"

"That isn't his stage name."

"Yeah, right — he's the real Plato! And the other guy is Buddha."

Keith grinned.

The *Plato*…

As part of his psychology studies he'd read a digested introduction to philosophers. He'd been particularly impressed by the early Greek thinkers; he found it hard to fathom that so many of their concepts were still relevant almost two and a half thousand years later. He sometimes wondered if anything he ever said would be worthwhile repeating just a couple of hours later.

"How can I make it up to Plato?"

"When you stop pigeonholing him, you might want to pay him another visit."

"I was rude. What an idiot."

"He'll forgive you."

He had to forgive himself first.

"Don't worry, I've already had a chat with him."

"You're a good friend, Keith. Are we allowed to be friends after your official work is done?"

Keith glowed. Peter guessed being a priest had been a lonely path and as an Arrival Angel, most relationships were probably transient. The guy was growing on him.

"Sure we can be friends," said Keith throwing an arm around Peter's shoulders. "Besides, you're a great wingman." Keith laughed and gave him a light jab on the arm.

He tried to ignore him then rolled with the joke, flapping his free arm like a chicken wing. Keith's laughter roared a few more decibels then he flapped his free arm in unison and Peter broke out in laughter too.

⌒～⌒

PETER scurried into Plato's den in H.E.L.L., determined to make things right but he stopped just inside the entrance when he saw Plato playing table soccer. With the same intensity.

Plato…

Buddha meditated on a wide bench next to the atrium wall. Despite his eagerness to apologize, he didn't want to interrupt either of them. Being in the presence of the actual Plato and Buddha was intimidating; unfamiliar territory. Weird on weird.

When Plato stopped playing he stared ahead and nodded. He wasn't sure if Plato was contemplating the game he just finished or a philosophical insight. When Plato looked across,

Peter squirted out his words like water from a high pressure hose.

"I'm really sorry for what I said last time. It's been a confusing week. I thought I came here to find my dad in Hell but I guess it was just a diversion because I had to work out my soulmate and didn't know how to do that, and I ended up projecting my anger at you."

Plato studied him.

He held his breath for what felt like hours.

"Who are you?" said Plato.

"Peter. Your friend, Keith, brought me here a week ago."

Plato raised his hand and slowly moved to him. "No." Plato placed his hand over Peter's heart; he was drawn deep into Plato's tunnel eyes again. "Who are you? Until you know this, you cannot connect with your soulmate."

Who am I?

At first they were just three tiny words floating around deep in his mind, searching for relevance, a connection. He closed his eyes and the question echoed louder and louder.

"Until you know this, you cannot connect with your soulmate."

From his mom, to Christina, to Jane, he'd been something of a chameleon; almost following his own path but usually just happy to be nudged along by these great women. This week he was further away from his own center than ever. Bouncing between Jane and Christina… then his mom… and Christina and Jane.

How can I know my soulmate if I don't truly know me? Chris is on her path. Jane too.

"Boo!" Buddha yelled.

He jumped.

Buddha laughed loud.

"I must apologize. My buddy, Buddha, thinks he is great comedian. Maybe because he is his best audience," said Plato.

Buddha laughed louder.

Peter smiled. Crazy and surreal, but he was so glad he came back.

Buddha settled down. "The search begins with you."

He was transfixed by Buddha's eyes, sparkling so much he couldn't make out the color.

"Plato believes you should never give up hope of finding your other half."

He nodded, his inner-world calmer.

"Buddha believes you should not long for anyone," said Plato.

How do you not long for someone while never giving up on finding them?

"Your destiny lies somewhere between the two," said Buddha.

Peter was definitely confused.

Buddha laughed then stilled himself with an intensity matching Plato's. "Forget wisdom. You listen inside." He patted his heart. "Rest is easy."

Plato put one hand on Peter's shoulder and pointed with his other towards the reading area below.

"There is one letter you must read. Maybe it helps you."

"A letter? From who?"

"Your wife."

Plato guided him out. Peter shuffled along the landing, still in a haze with the conflicting advice. Advice on a subject he hadn't intended covering. As he reached the stairs heading down to the reading area, he stopped and grabbed the rail tightly.

A letter from my wife? Which wife?

He skipped down the stairs, chasing his heightened curiosity.

Magic Wands

Weird.

PETER read the date at the top of the letter again; written six months after Christina died, yet in her unmistakable scrawl.

The cubicle glowed blue around the white light from the reading lamp. A glass cover encased the letter to preserve its longevity; quivering hands created a strobe affect with the lamplight flickering into his eyes off the glass. He laid the letter on the table and took a long breath. It had always been impossible to revisit Christina's death without his stomach and heart shriveling up like dried-out old sponges.

"Listen inside. Rest is easy."

Easy for Buddha to say.

His eyes did one more loop between "My Gorgeous Peter" and the date before he took a deep breath and read the letter.

"My Gorgeous Peter,

Hell, I miss you. Can't begin to imagine the pain you've been going through. I wish there was some way to let you know about this place — that eventually we can be together again. First day here I was listening to a busker next to the river where we met and the pain was so intense I collapsed. Some kind people brought me here, to H.E.L.L.

Perfect!

Plato tried to make me feel better. He said if we're meant to be together, we'll have an eternity to reconnect when you die, but that could take sixty years and right now another six months feels like an eternity!!!

I go to our spot on the river every day without collapsing now. Do you remember the song you were playing before I 'tripped' over your case? Kinda spooky how much those words make sense now. The way you teased that song through your guitar still ripples through me every time I sit there.

A part of me wishes you can move on and find someone to love again; someone who will love you too. You deserve that. But a much huger part of me can't stand the thought of you with another woman. How twisted is that?

Oh yeah, you're probably wondering why I quit my teaching job the day I died? It's your fault!!! The courage you showed in following your music dreams inspired me. I was rushing home to tell you I was going to set up my own mechanic shop. Yes, me! Thanks to sweet, gorgeous you. I wanted you to be the first to know. That's why I didn't see the car that hit me. Oh, the poor driver. I hope he gets through this OK. I hope you don't blame him, Peter. It wasn't his fault. I just didn't look, it was wet, he didn't have a chance.

I can't wait to see you up here. I can't wait to hear about all your amazing gigs and the music you've created.

Live your life Peter. In full Peter-style!!!

Your crazy wife,

Christina.

PS: It takes a while to get used to the heightened emotional thing we have Up Here. It's a real rollercoaster sometimes. But then you realize it focuses you on what really matters, like a magnifying glass on your feelings. It filters out all the stuff that's trivial. If I had a second chance down there I'd spend more time meditating and walking or just sitting. Stop laughing! I can learn to sit still and meditate.

The one thing now that is painfully clear to me is how much you mattered, Peter. You were like my emotional magnifying glass. You never judged or lectured. You knocked down negative doors inside me that I always had a big lock on. And the sweetest, most loving thing about all that was you didn't even know you did it. You just accepted me and my crazy dreams. My crazy ways.

And I've got an even bigger, crazier dream now. I hope I can make it work before you make it Up Here.

PPS: (is that how they write it, or is it meant to be PSS?) I love you, Peter Christian and no matter what happens when you get Up Here, I will always love you."

Peter slumped back in the chair, overwhelmed; not with pain, just wonderful warm emotions he didn't think he'd feel again after the catastrophe in his driveway.

Am I Ever Gonna See Your Face Again, The Angels rock classic that he'd played the way Doc Neeson originally wrote it; a haunting ballad about his friend's grief after his girlfriend died in a motorcycle accident. That's what he was playing when he met Christina. The lyric could have been written for him after her death.

What a letter.

The Christina Dimadis junior high school biology teacher who hated writing, who especially struggled to express anything remotely personal. The Christina who handed in a five hundred word uni essay with exactly five hundred words, not one extra syllable. The woman who never scribbled more than the standard few words on Christmas and birthday cards. That Christina wrote this.

Wow-mazing.

Red light washed over him inside the booth. He looked up to see Plato and Buddha on the walkway that circled the vast reading room, nodding. Their work was done now. The rest was up to him.

❧

Throughout his walkabout downtown, one sentence from Christina's letter kept swirling around PETER'S head.

"The courage you showed in following your music dreams inspired me."

I inspired her? Chris was my muse; she inspired me! And now, unknowingly, with a letter she wrote almost nine years ago, she's guiding me again.

He couldn't recall deciding to end up at their spot, staring at the Yarra River, but he could retrace his steps. He was sure that the best way to *"listen inside"* and make sense of the other nuggets of advice from Plato and Buddha was to not work hard at it. He needed fresh air and he also had to let Christina's letter breathe inside him.

He had swung back down the Paris end of Collins St; the collision of heritage buildings, modern skyscrapers, imposing churches, five-star hotels and designer shops all somehow colluded to create a beautiful architectural montage. The plane trees formed a guard of honor for the trams and horse carriages. He was glad to see Haigh's Chocolates still there. This sweet spot was one of the few happy memories with his dad. He ducked in and bought a packet of his favorite milk chocolate frogs.

Many lanes and a few hours later he ended his pilgrimage on the banks of the river where he and Christina met, unplanned and inevitable, and sat at the table where she so elegantly showed him with gelato that three into a space for two didn't work.

He bit off the head of a chocolate frog and let it melt for a bit in his mouth but he could never resist chomping in to it quickly. One thing he remembered from his dad, because he repeated it so often in their short time together.

"There isn't a problem in the world that chocolate can't solve, Pete."

He doesn't believe his dad made up the mantra but it always stuck. Maybe it wasn't at the level of a Plato or Buddha but, at the very least, it provided an excuse to eat chocolate.

"The courage you showed in following your music dreams inspired me."

Why did this line keep floating back into his mind? The longer he meditated on the flowing river, the more the line bubbled to the surface. Eventually he realized it was the other way around; the thought came from deep inside him. It was always there, but he was listening to it now.

Who am I? Plato had challenged him. *Who am I?*

Not just a husband; and definitely not given this soul

simply to develop wannabe leaders, like the work he did with Glen. He'd absolved his responsibility to himself. His own life purpose. Without that, how could he be the man who Jane or Christina deserved? If he wasn't following his path, how could he know who else's path was aligned with his?

Glen often challenged leadership participants with a question: "If you had a magic wand and money was no object but you still had to work or be productive, what would you do?"

Up Here everyone was handed an eternal magic wand, a new beginning with nothing to lose. It had taken a while to get his head around that.

By the time he'd devoured seven chocolate frogs, one clear idea nibbled at him. He had his own magic wands at home, both beautifully crafted with six-strings. Whether they were a means, or an end, he wasn't sure. He certainly wasn't going to find out by using them as dust collectors.

Unofficially, JANE didn't have to prove her suitability to foster Laura. Uniting Children assured her everyone at Harpo House raved about her natural intuition with children, including the most traumatized children. But she still had to go through a process before being allowed the privilege of taking Laura home as her foster-mom.

Like so many aspects of Up Here, Jane was impressed with the process, a simple, unique piece of child empathy not based on the usual bureaucratic formalities.

A panel of three parents and two independent therapists observed her remotely through cameras as she spent time with Laura. Her objective was to find out pieces of backstory on Laura that would help any relationship going forward; stuff you wouldn't find in official files.

Children don't tend to answer direct questions, certainly not a barrage of them, so she engaged Laura in games, readings and craft activities whilst extracting bits of Laura's life and preferences. Jane's biggest challenge, like most adults in this situation, was to avoid second-guessing how she was supposed to act.

That danger flew out the window as soon as Laura had skipped into the room. Her clinical psychologist's brain was instantly and involuntarily pushed aside by Laura's presence and personality.

Apparently she'd never had any music lessons and now wanted to be a "per-cush-est". Jane could blame Peter for this future noisy rumble.

Laura loved apples. Not the ugly green ones, the shiny, stripy, super-sweet red ones. She was allowed to go to bed really, really late: seven-thirty. Jane gave Laura's parents a secret big tick on that one.

Her favorite teacher was Miss Ashley, "coz she always sang in the morning and after lunch when they walked into class." Her favorite book was *The Cat in the Hat* because her dad read it with silly voices.

It was a productive few sessions, but more importantly, Jane had fun. No matter what happened with Peter down the eternal track, she had to follow this path with Laura.

The panel entrusted with the decision agreed Laura would be in loving, capable hands. Jane had to contain her elation until she was sure of Laura's reaction. Sitting on a small classroom chair, she tentatively explained the situation to Laura. The stillness on Laura's face gave no hint of emotion, nothing Jane could hang her comfort on. After what seemed like an hour but was just seconds, Laura broke the silence.

"You mean like being my mom?"

"Yes. Just until your mom and dad make it Up Here."

Laura stared blankly.

Jane swallowed hard.

Laura's smile spread across her whole face, sparking a wonderful fire inside Jane. Laura hugged her tight and she hugged back with all the love in her soul. A tear rolled off her face onto Laura's shoulder.

The blast from the three-piece horn section spun PETER back to the present. The Nat Empire rehearsal was in full swing and he'd frozen inside the Spiegeltent entrance with his guitars either side.

What was I thinking? These musos aren't a band, they're a carnival.

He loved the venue and had never seen it empty. Hand-built in Belgium about one hundred years ago, the circular design was surrounded by red velvet and mirrored walls, booths, bars and a stage.

Nat's vocals were spine-tingling, while Erica supported and played trumpet. Apart from the funky horn section, they had an amazing keyboard player, double bass, drummer and a DJ scratching records.

Look at Nat move! I should go, maybe find another band.

He picked up his guitar cases to sneak back out before anyone saw him. Too late.

Erica waved Peter towards the stage without missing a note, playing one-handed on her trumpet.

Peter joined them, plugged in his Harrison and listened for a while. His feet always caught the vibe first, right boot tapped to the rhythm, launching the soundwaves through his body, demanding a release via his fingers. He strummed a few chords. Nat gave him a thumbs up, Erica dipped her head on an angle and winked. The longer Peter played, the deeper he buried those nerves, the more he swung into their groove. The other band members slowly nodded their acceptance as they enjoyed his licks.

Zen-zone.

Immersed in the moment, at one with the music, his guitar and the high-energy band members who were giving everything they had, despite it being just a rehearsal. James Jamerson, the gifted Motown bass player once said, "If you can't feel it, don't play it." Peter knew no other way on stage and The Nat Empire took it to another dimension.

It wasn't just the buzz of playing again; he loved the collaboration. Bouncing off talented musos and finding unexpected creative sweet spots, including some silly antics along the way. What a blast. He was in his element. No thoughts, just feeling; a glorious warm energy oozed into him through his guitar.

JANE admired the way Christina fiddled with the engine in her Mustang, intensity with a smile. She was proud of

Christina, how she'd followed her dreams and created her own little nirvana Up Here.

Sennasation was closed and the light hanging over the opened bonnet on the end of a long lead gave Christina an angelic look. She knew this angel could turn fiery demon in a split second and hoped her gesture would help them get back on the friendship road.

When she had the wonderful news about Laura confirmed, a hollow sadness followed her initial elation. Her natural course of action would have been to immediately call Christina, share her special moment and celebrate together with an impromptu Chinese meal and lots of Pinot Gris. The hesitation driven by their recent Peter-chasm hurt. After a few rounds of internal kickboxing, Jane phoned Christina, who'd sounded genuinely delighted about the news.

Laura had unknowingly become the catalyst to realigning their lifetime friendship. Talking on the phone was one thing; being in the same space after everything they'd been through was another, which is why she'd brought a gift.

Christina reached to the bench for a spanner then stopped and straightened with a grin that could go humor or attack. Christina pointed the large spanner at what Jane was holding; flat, about one yard by one and a half, covered in a cloth.

"Doesn't look like a weapon," Christina said.

She smiled. Christina's humor had always been the lubricant of their friendship. When life had thrown boulders or craters in her path and Jane analyzed options to death, it was Christina the jester whose laughter always brought things down to a balanced earth, yanking Jane back into the moment.

"Wish I could say the same," she said, pointing at the spanner in Christina's hand.

Christina's grin morphed into a full welcome smile. She put down the spanner and wiped her hands on her coveralls. Jane stood her gift up on the workbench and unwrapped the cloth to reveal a framed painting of Christina's Mustang. The number plate: CHRISTINA 1.

Christina caught her breath and covered her mouth with her hands. Maybe she saw tears, but Christina quickly turned and walked away.

Jane was disappointed. Confused.

Christina walked to a corner of the shed, taking the light on the long power lead with her. She pulled back a small tarp and rolled forward a shiny red Mustang-replica go-kart. It featured the number plate: LAURA 1

Jane's hand spread across her heart as joyous energy swirled through. Not just because of the beautiful creative gift; if their friendship could survive the last week, it could survive anything. She stepped towards Christina who met her halfway with arms wide. Jane's arms didn't need a second invitation as she hugged her tight.

"If I could choose a mom, I'd choose you too," said Christina.

She pulled back and wiped a tear with her long sleeve. "And if I could choose a sister, I'd choose you."

Christina buried her head in her shoulder. "I'd have to be the older one or you'd dominate the hell out of me."

She laughed. "You were always stronger."

"Yeah, but now you have two full arms." Christina quivered, giggling under her arms.

At Sennasation next morning, in between sipping coffees and munching on donuts, all the crew admired the painting of Christina's Mustang hanging proudly over her workbench. They'd never heard of an artist named Doctor Jane.

CHRISTINA smiled at the cheeky touch by her soul sister.

One of the guys joked it would have been perfect with a blonde in tight shorts and wet singlet lying across the bonnet. She landed her spanner on his toe from five meters. He fell over from the surprise, his coffee and donut flying cross the workshop. They all laughed.

For PETER, the melody always came first.

For some it was a riff, others a drum and bass beat, or a chord progression. For the multitalented show-offs, words popped out with the melody.

Gut feeling told him the pop-dance track he'd created was good. Surprisingly good, considering how long his creative juices had been left in the freezer.

Huddled over his pen and A4-pad at his studio mixing desk, the blue ink lines and shadings from his doodles dominated the page, almost covering what he'd written. He'd been struggling with words for the hook, the catchy, syrupy core of any pop song.

He was close.

"When I'm with you" was scribbled under the heading, "CHORUS'. There was a gap with lines drawn for three elusive words. The breeding doodles threatened to take over that precious space. Three simple syllables to complete the meter. But they couldn't be just any words. They had to say something.

The rest of the chorus and the verses were all down. As often happened with inspiration, his post-Nat Empire high didn't have enough fuel to finish what he'd started. They had invited him to join the band on stage at their performance tomorrow. Tomorrow!

Focus, Peter, focus. Maybe scrap the first four words. "When I'm with you" is hardly original. Why did I say yes? It was just one rehearsal. I'm a basic pop-rock dude, they're masters of jazz and gypsy and pop and reggae and Latin; and they can really play! I should be practicing.

He hit a button on his desk and the catchy melody bounced out of the Yamaha monitors. He closed his eyes and flowed with the music… let the words come… the melody line built up as it reached the chorus and… nothing. Not even three silly words to fill up the spaces, which was the usual process when things weren't flowing.

He needed time away from his creative wall. He left the pen on the pad, downloaded the music track onto his phone then shut the mixing desk. He slung the Harrison over his shoulder like an F1 driver slips into a customized cockpit. He had to play anything but his new track or music remotely close to The Nat Empire. Without making a conscious decision, his fingers set off on the opening riff of his favorite Springsteen tune, *Born to Run.*

Two boys ran either side of Laura in her shiny new go-kart as she swerved along the downhill paved path. The joy on her face burst through her helmet.

JANE smiled from her office window.

She went back to her desk and resumed her online search for houses nearby; roomy enough inside for two, with a yard big enough to entertain an adventurous little girl.

An electric reverberation through the amp startled PETER awake. He'd dozed off on the couch with the guitar on his lap but it had slipped onto the floor. The melody of his new song rolled through his head unprompted.

Good sign.

He grabbed the page of lyrics next to him, waiting for the inspiration to pour out… and as the melody hit the chorus… nothing. A lyrical black hole. He folded it up and put it in his pocket with a pen. Writing had to take a backseat for the day.

While he carefully packed and re-packed each guitar in its case with picks, cables and cleaning cloths, he had been mulling over his three missions for the day. First his mom, followed by the gig. But it was a battle to not be consumed by the third mission: confirming his soulmate. Because when he finally faced his own "magic wand" question, it became clear the process led to two connected answers.

"If you had a magic wand and you could do anything, but still had to work, what would you do?"

He was now sure of his path and the moment his clarity clicked, so did his other half, his soulmate. As his favorite new gurus had suggested, he didn't have any longing. There was simply a comfortable *knowing*.

Faith

PETER wasn't sure what to expect at the Faith Village. He'd urged his mom to meet somewhere else but she'd insisted. As he checked out the oval space while he waited for her outside the Catholic Church, he was glad she had.

A large lawn area, about the size of five tennis courts side by side, was surrounded with flowers, shrubs, walking paths and wooden tables and chairs. Outside the perimeter garden, people walked in and out of temples and churches of various religions and faiths. Between a mosque and synagogue, Muslim men and women chatted and laughed with male and female rabbis and other Jews; some in their traditional dress, including hijabs, burqas and kippas, but many were in non-religious clothes from a range of eras.

A Christian priest bowled a red rubber ball to a Hindu man wielding a cricket bat, as monks, Indian, Pakistani and Anglo-Saxon kids prepared to catch the ball. Black Africans played soccer with Hare Krishnas, Aboriginals, an Orthodox priest,

Asian people and a bunch of other multicultural Aussies.

Under a towering ghost gum tree at one end, an Aboriginal Elder had a large group of children mesmerized with a story. As his hands swayed, the children's heads swayed left, then right and up then down. In between the Mormon and Seventh-day Adventist churches, a few hippies straight from a late-sixties or early seventies poster, led a crazy dance with immaculately groomed women, men and children in dark suits and dresses. Uninhibited fun and laughter bubbled everywhere.

Surrounded by the happy, peaceful energy, he also sensed a different kind of inner calm. A blunting of the edge that subliminally became an inescapable part of everyone's DNA on Earth; where he was bombarded with images and stories of violence, war and fear for the environment. Social media, smartphones and super-fast internet spat all the negativity at him faster, everywhere. But Up Here his muscles, tendons and bones were lying on beach chairs while his heart and organs floated in the shallows; the undercurrent tension from Earth on a permanent holiday.

The hum of people talking dragged Peter out of his sunny thoughts. The big church doors were wide open and a female priest said goodbye to people as they thanked her for the sermon. He did a double-take and checked the front banner to make sure he wasn't outside the wrong church. No, definitely Catholic.

His mom's cackle slipped through the church doors before she did. It took dying to help him understand how much her love had shaped his life; giving him the belief to be whoever he wanted, and the strength to get through whatever obstacles were thrown at him. He would never have had the confidence to be with two amazing women like Christina and Jane if it wasn't for his mom.

Linda smiled when she saw him. "That's my handsome son." She pointed for the priest. The priest waved at him and he waved back at her.

Linda joined him at the bottom of the steps.

"Female Catholic priest?" said Peter.

"Uh-huh," said Linda without a hint of pride, like it was the norm.

A man stepped out with a young boy and girl. He kissed the priest affectionately on the lips, then they both said goodbye to the departing congregation. Their kids ran off to join in the cricket match.

"Her husband and family," said Linda.

He looked around the Faith Village. "This isn't what I imagined."

"Beautiful, isn't it? It's not like love is in the air, more like love is the air."

"Speaking of love, these are for all the times I never listened to you." He handed her the bunch of Sundaze Bronze daisies. "And for everything you had to go through to raise me." Words and flowers could never fully thank his mom for all the years she struggled to bring him up on her own. How could you possibly thank the person who was so determined to give him life?

"Thank you."

"Nothing special."

"It's always special when someone goes to the trouble of picking out a beautiful bunch of nature's smiles, just for you."

She kissed him on the cheek. "You remembered my favorites too."

"Speaking of favorites, about your shop…"

"Yes."

"Well… your window display is beautiful, but… you deserve a male mannequin."

Her eyes went all mushy. "Any particular male mannequin?"

"Some mannequins are fragile… you have to be gentle with him. I mean them." After the initial shock of how he found out about Keith and his Mom, the idea of the two of them linking up romantically had grown on him.

Linda smiled, then hugged him. "I'm so proud of you."

"I'm proud of you too, Mom."

She squeezed his cheek. "Ready for your gig?"

He pulled her hand down. "No. And it's not my gig, I'm just helping out on a couple of songs."

"You are ready." She turned and yelled across the Faith Village. "My boy is going to be a rock star!"

The priest behind them started clapping and she was joined by many of the other adults around the village.

"Seriously, Mom!"

"You are a star, Peter. Enjoy the moment."

"You're sure she'll be there?"

"She'll be there."

"I love you, Mom."

"I love you, Peter. Now break a leg, or guitar string, or whatever they say in rock and roll."

He walked backwards and grinned. "They say this." He raised his hand in the classic rock-salute, pointer finger and little finger sticking out, thumb across the two closed fingers. Linda rock-saluted right back at him. Some of the gang around the Faith Village rock-saluted too… he saluted them as well… within a few steps everyone was rock-saluting. Women in Burqas, men in kippas and children doing it with both hands.

PETER heard Christina's distinctive piercing whistle during the applause after his first number and managed to avoid looking in her direction. There were important plans after the show, but first he had to repay the spirit of generosity The Nat Empire had shown him. He'd been a little self-conscious during the first song, even though the packed house had given him a raucous welcome when he was introduced. By the end of the song he was definitely in the groove.

During the final song, the crowd frenzy grew as he answered the challenge from Theo the keyboardist, in a ridiculous mini-musical battle. Unrehearsed and unplanned, they alternately raised the stakes with an increasingly difficult riff. The rest of the band encouraged them with little additions but they were almost part of the crowd as they enjoyed the inspired musical moment that can only happen at a live gig. Natalie even ran off stage to grab her phone and record the duel on video. It was one of those events where three thousand people in years to come would claim to be part of the three hundred in the crowd.

During that last song, he finally looked at Christina while Theo played a physics-defying sequence with his back to the keyboard. Sweet déjà vu; they could have been at any of his early gigs with Christina lost in his music. Her wild curly hair was the only dancing partner that could keep up. The full length black dress with deep purple patterns accentuated her flowing river bend moves, moves that attracted every male gaze and a few female admirers too.

When he locked eyes, she instinctively raised her hand in a rock salute. He saluted back. Christina kept her hand in rock salute form but brought her pointer finger to her nose, stuck it in a little and swiveled her hand; her fun ego-squashing reminder. He laughed, then copied her on stage. Christina laughed.

The drummer kicked in, ending the keyboard versus guitar dual. Peter and Theo high-fived and bowed as the crowd erupted in wild appreciation, then the band spiraled into a feverish finale.

"Thank you, thank you. You've all been brilliant. Love and peace, love and peace," said a breathless Natalie, before the band joined hands at the front of the stage and bowed for the crowd.

Peter was riding such a high he could've kissed every member of the audience, but he only blew a kiss to one before running off stage with the band. Christina.

CHRISTINA led the crowd as they chanted, clapped and stomped, demanding The Nat Empire encore magic. Or maybe she just wanted to see Peter on stage again. Getting that blown kiss from him was a throwback to a much simpler time, when she was the only woman in the world that mattered. The only woman he'd invite backstage. The only woman he'd married.

She could barely control the flutter of warmth when Linda first told her about Peter performing again. It took all her concentration to not let it overwhelm her. She'd started the night sipping beers in a rear booth with Linda, keen to support Peter but didn't want to go overboard. She'd decided to be there as a supportive friend for Peter and keep Linda company. A solid plan… until the music started. Her inner-rush took over and she dragged Linda through the crowd, close to the stage.

Keith's laser-attention from the side of the stage on Linda was so cute. Like a virginal teenager, every time Linda looked his way his eyes whiplashed away. In her white Nancy Sinatra boots, short denim skirt and black blouse, Linda lapped it up and shimmied with an X-factor G-force.

Now the show was over she glanced between the stage exits for signs of Peter, but he surprised her in the pit, taking her hand and weaving her through the throng to backstage where it was marginally quieter.

His hand was warm, too warm. She let go.

Peter did the rock salute nose pick. "Do you remember the first time you did that?"

"Your first gig at the Espy."

"I still can't believe you did that at the Espy."

"I can't believe you did it on stage." She remembered the zany prank like it happened yesterday.

Peter's black t-shirt was soaked in perspiration, but his wavy hair looked as playful as ever. She saw enough of his tight black jeans when he was on stage and didn't dare look down now, still feeling the heat from his hand.

"I'm so glad you came."

"You really rocked, Pete. You belong up there."

"Thanks. It's so obvious now. Music is my thing. And you're the only one who believed in me. You always believed in me, more than I did."

She wanted to hug him… run away… kiss him… run further.

"Chris, we are soulmates."

She'd been desperate to hear those words for nine years, yet she couldn't embrace them. "You're on a high right now. When you come down from your rock 'n roll rush you'll—"

"Just hold me and we'll never be able to let go," he held his arms wide.

She stepped back; not prepared for this. Not Peter's intent, not his challenge, not the warmth flowing through her. She couldn't edge towards that cliff again. She turned to flee.

"I read your letter."

She stopped and searched Peter's eyes.

That letter!

"Nat Empire, Nat Empire," the crowd chanted melodically.

"That was a long time ago, Pete," Christina said. "I'm different now."

"You're better now. You're more you now than when we were together."

Peter stepped forward. Her heart didn't allow her to step back, although her spirit demanded she make a sprint for the Mustang.

"Chris, this time I really know. We don't have to fight it. It's right." Peter held her hands. "Our paths are linked. Always have been, always will be."

A jumble of thoughts bounced around her mind to the thumping in her heart and she had to look down. There, she found her escape route.

She lifted his wrist and pointed out the wedding band on his finger.

"Does Jane know?"

Peter's face switched from glowing to grimace. He fiddled with the platinum ring.

"I was planning to tell her straight after the gig," he said. "Come with me right now. Please."

Groundhog Day. She'd been around this map too many times the last couple of weeks and didn't enjoy any of the trips. She couldn't do it this way; shook her head then rushed for the door.

"Chris!"

She took off, risking one quick glance over her shoulder at the rear door. Peter struggled to pierce the crowd.

Good.

CHRISTINA dived into her Mustang and fired up the engine, revved hard, put it in gear and was about to release the handbrake.

"Where are you going?"

Linda leaning on the passenger door, casual, no edge.

Christina stared ahead. She hadn't addressed that minor issue. This journey was driven by what she had to leave, not where she had to go. "Nowhere."

"I definitely know the directions to that place," said Linda.

On one hand, Linda had been her best friend the last nine years. On the other hand, she was a direct link to Peter. And right now, she was determined to push Peter out of her mind. She couldn't take any more of that romantic rollercoaster.

Yet something deep inside whispered.

Friendship first.

She indicated with a slight jerk of her head for Linda to get in. Linda hurdled the door, landing on the passenger seat. She floored the accelerator and the Mustang fishtailed out of the carpark. In the rearview mirror she caught a glimpse of Peter running out of the door, followed by Keith.

JANE watched the ducks search for food on the Harpo House pond. She loved this secluded little haven, hidden from the rest of the children's play areas by drooping willow trees that tickled the reeds. She wasn't surprised about the drooping inside her. Ending any relationship was never easy, even when it was the right decision.

She stroked the lush green grass then massaged her shoeless foot. It had been good to hear Peter's voice on the phone earlier. He seemed in a good place, despite being overly careful about his words. Such a sensitive soul.

It also confirmed for her, not that she needed more confirming, she'd made the right choice. Having the opportunity to be a mother to Laura, rather than just therapist to many children, had fulfilled a deep yearning she never would have predicted. The surprising joy when she thought she was pregnant had unleashed a powerful force that hadn't waned.

The few months Up Here, even the last few weeks with Peter, only helped to clarify being a mother was more important than any romantic relationship. Jane's clinical and normally dominant brain was relegated to follow the evolution as a spectator. No biological ticking clock, just a raw, soulful desire to intimately connect with and raise a little Soul; to create a psychological, emotional and spiritual umbilical cord.

A shadow made her turn. Peter held a gift bag and a dozen red roses. A smile slipped its way through; how could she ever forget the last roses Peter brought to her bath? She admired their deep red hue and slowly inhaled the sweet perfume, before placing the roses on the ground between them.

She enjoyed the peacefulness with Peter beside her, silence of a non-school day added to the serenity. Three ducks paddled over, probably hoping this new big arrival on the lofty bank had bought some food scraps for them. When they realized there was no bread miracle from Peter, they paddled away.

PETER hadn't been looking forward to the conversation. Because he loved Jane. He just knew that Christina was his soulmate. He'd never truly explored the notion of soulmates when they were together first time round. He never had to. He'd also never had to end a relationship with someone he truly loved. Someone with whom he'd shared so much.

After the Spiegeltent moment with Christina he'd rushed home, showered, replaced his black t-shirt and jeans, with a white t-shirt and blue jeans and made the call.

Jane placed her left hand on his right hand. He raised her hand to kiss it, noticing Jane wasn't wearing her engagement and wedding rings.

Maybe Jane heard it in my voice. Maybe she…

Jane saw him staring at her naked ring finger and took the original burgundy ring box out of her handbag, as well as a letter-sized document, folded in three. He read the official confirmation that Jane had become the foster-mom for Laura.

His stomach unknotted, releasing a warm flush of happiness for Jane. When she told him on the phone she also had something to share with him, he wasn't sure what would come out in this delicate moment. They'd both found their paths and they weren't aligned. That made things a little easier.

He gave her back the letter and kissed her cheek. Jane opened the ring box and her rings were in their place. He removed his wedding ring, kissed it tenderly then put it in a vacant slot in the box. Jane closed the box, kissed it then put it back in her bag.

"You'll be a great mom."

"I had plenty of practice with you."

He smiled and passed the gift bag to her. Her eyes expanded as wide as the tambourine she pulled out. She banged it a couple of times and pretended to bang it on his head. She hugged him instead.

"She'll love it." Jane put it back in the bag then pulled the head off one of the roses. "This is for opening my heart. Without your love I may never have realized how much I wanted to be a mother. It took a special archaeologist to dig that deep, to brush the dust off so delicately." Jane kissed the rose head, placed it in the water and gave it a gentle push. The ducks scampered back to check what was on the easy menu then skulked away again.

Jane pulled off another rose head. "This is for being so brave and making me laugh when I was terrified of dying." She kissed the rose head and repeated the sendoff.

He pulled off a rose head. "This is for helping me live and love again when I thought my heart died with Christina." He repeated the ritual.

Jane pulled off two rose heads. "And these are for you and…" Jane shifted her head to that angle. "How much you will look after Christina."

He smiled at Jane's caring tone for Christina. More proof they had both chosen the right course. He pulled off two rose heads. "And these are for the wonderful adventures you will have with Laura."

Jane pulled off a rose head. "This is for never singing me a cheesy love song again."

He pulled off another one. "And this is for never having to go to another bloody opera."

Jane kissed Peter's cheek, slowly, gently. He put his arm around her and she rested her head on his shoulder. He knew they had some grieving to work through, but he also knew they would always have a special place in each other's hearts. As they watched the bobbing rose heads drift away, the history of their relationship rippled across the pond; lovers, partners, spouses and eternal special friends.

When I'm With You

The Great Ocean Road, my Mustang and me — that's my kind of love triangle. Everyone belongs. No one gets hurt.

CHRISTINA loved the wild flapping of her hair, the exhilaration of speeding just inches from cliffs and the inner-rush through G-force bends. With the roof rolled down, the salty air and stunning vistas blasted her senses like waves crashing on the rocks below.

Like a dog in a Ute. Peter might have created her epitaph.

She didn't want to think about him or his rendezvous with Jane, which meant she couldn't stop thinking about him.

Peter had sounded clear and genuine. She couldn't argue with anything he'd said in the Spiegeltent. That's why she was driving. The further she drove, the further she'd be away from any potential bad news. Whatever positive notions her instincts were whispering about Peter and Jane and Laura, she couldn't help feeling that some unexpected detour could pop up at any time that threw all intuition and logic over the cliff.

She had an internal chuckle when she realized she was driving along the shipwreck coast. Perfect.

She didn't have a mobile and neither did Linda. After she'd been Up Here a few years and got into the flow of eternity, mobile phones became superfluous. She was grateful that Linda had honored the silence. More than a good friend, Linda was her Earth mother. Christina did love her parents and was looking forward to that reunion but she had uprooted forever from their tightly controlled garden. Up Here, Linda had become her sun, her water, her fertilizer. She wondered about hugging the road all the way to the Twelve Apostles… maybe even Warrnambool.

"Hey, Thelma," shouted Linda.

Christina smiled and for a split second considered driving off the cliff like the seminal moment in *Thelma and Louise*, the movie that helped them consume more popcorn and beer in each other's lounge rooms than any other. Driving off a cliff Up Here had become an irresistible rite of passage for many BFFs, male and female. But not in her Mustang, not today.

"Maybe it's time to head back," said Linda.

She focused on the sharp bend, found a line that allowed minimal braking, came out of the apex smooth then rammed the accelerator again.

"My gut feeling is positive. Things are going to work out for you," said Linda.

"Your gut feeling is always positive for me."

"Sometimes the further you go, the less you leave."

She shot Linda a glance.

"Bend!" screamed Linda.

She slid the Mustang sideways around the bend then focused on the road ahead.

"The further you go the less you leave."

She wished Linda wasn't so wise. After another wordless kilometer, she accepted Linda's prodding and slowed down during a straight stretch, just enough to do a speedy hand-brake turn using up every bit of the tight two-lane bitumen.

Linda shrieked, gripping the door and dashboard.

When the car was almost straight again she peeked at Linda, whose smile beamed as wide as the windscreen; the woman loved every daredevil second. Pushing each other out of comfort zones was a mutual treat. They headed back to Melbourne at Christina's standard cruising speed: fast.

PETER paced outside Sennasation, checking the time on his phone. After his sad but friendly goodbye with Jane he'd needed time to regroup, so he'd walked there. While Peter always enjoyed walking, one of the added advantages Up Here was he never got physically tired, so walking made more sense than ever. But Christina wasn't around, or answering her phone, and waiting for everyone pushed his patience

There was no logic to his haste. He knew they had an eternity but that knowledge didn't dilute the urgency inside him, the turbo-charged pining. Once he had worked out who his soulmate was, he needed to confirm the feeling was mutual as quickly as possible.

After nine years apart, all he wanted was to be with Christina.

A car horn startled him. He didn't recognize the car and was about to yell at the driver, but then Keith got out.

"She's not here. We have to…" He took in Keith, grinning like a new moon beside the shiny blue car. "Wow, you bought a gentleman's sports car."

"Hah, very good. Gentlemen and shining knights," said Keith.

"Trust me, no self-respecting knight would shine in this. But it is a looker."

"Yes, it looks much faster than it is." Keith paraded around his new toy. Peter also noticed Keith's new white jeans, black shirt and boots and the floppy hairstyle. He was so nervous at his gig with so much to focus on, he hadn't noticed Keith's new appearance.

"You're having a mid-death crisis."

Keith smiled and did a slow spin with his arms wide.

Peter shook his head then was happily diverted by a truck with double passenger cabin arriving. Nat, Erica and the rest of The Nat Empire filed out. The three horn players stood up from their seats in the back tray section and played a funky little melody to announce their arrival. He ran over.

"Everyone back in, she's not here," he said.

"Oh man, we were hyped for the love," said Natalie.

The horn section did a little fizzle riff. He gave Natalie his mobile and played the new tune.

"You guys reckon you can learn this while you're driving?"

Nat and Erica nodded to the beat of the catchy pop-dance track. The drummer tapped the rhythm on the roof with his hands and the DJ threw in a couple of beatbox sounds.

"Sweet as," said Nat.

"Great, follow us."

He gave Nat the unfinished lyric and the band piled into the truck.

He ran back to Keith. "Give me the keys."

Keith hesitated. "I only picked it up yesterday."

"We have to find her now and I know how slow you drive."

"There's no rush, Peter. I don't understand."

"If you were torn away from your soulmate nine years ago and had the hellish couple of weeks I have and then you finally realize why she's your soulmate, you'd understand."

Keith's face morphed from serious to dreamy.

"I'm sure Linda's still with her."

Keith threw him the keys and slid into the passenger seat. "Hurry up. Let's go."

CHRISTINA still wasn't sure where she was heading.

Driving had always been a release and joy for her, its own reward, the destination often an afterthought. Back in the city she cruised the Mustang over the Westgate Bridge. With Port Melbourne and Port Phillip Bay shimmering to their right, the late afternoon sun reflected off the tall city buildings to the left.

"What happened at the Spiegeltent?" said Linda.

"Well, that's a record. Four whole hours before you minded my business."

Linda bit her lip.

"It's easier to love someone in your imagination. Reality is hard. And eternity is a long reality."

Linda nodded.

"We had our time. Everything has its time. Relationships, jobs, pets… eventually everything dies."

"Except love," said Linda.

She threw Linda a long glance.

"One way or another, love stays with you," Linda said. "Even if it had a bad ending, or bad moments, something good always comes out of love. You learn something about yourself, maybe about the world. It makes you wiser, or more understanding, or more grateful. Love never dies."

She let Linda's philosophical feathers float around her head. She wondered where Linda's wisdom on love came from. They certainly hadn't talked about it before. The words made a lot of sense but they still didn't relate specifically to her situation.

"Jane is smarter, more organized, she's good for him."

"Never picked you for one of those women who planted self-fulfilling prophecies in the backyard of doom."

"Now you're sounding like a magazine."

"Sounds like you're giving up."

"I'm not giving up. She replaced—"

"Jane didn't replace you, she replaced me."

She snapped her head towards Linda.

"Car… car!" yelled Linda, pointing ahead.

Christina swung the steering wheel hard right to avoid a slower car, then hard left again to avoid an oncoming car.

Linda let go of the dash and window frame. "I basically raised Peter on my own. Then he found you, which was wonderful. When you died, Peter was lost. He needed someone like Jane. I realize now she was good for him. I'm sure he loves her but not like he loves you."

"It hasn't felt that clear. He's obviously confused about us."

"Of course he was confused. What man wouldn't be in his situation? That doesn't mean you should add to his confusion."

A warmth seeped through the cracks Linda had found in her defensive walls.

"Or push him away because you're afraid," said Linda.

The walls collapsed. She was inundated with her love for Peter and needed to find him. Hold him. Linda's hand on her shoulder helped sober her into action.

She had a destination. "OK, first the Spiegeltent, in case he's still lingering in the afterglow of his comeback gig. If he's not there, just down the road is the spot on the Yarra where we met. It's amazing how many times we've ended up there, it's like our romantic pit-stop."

"Only you could make 'pit-stop' romantic. You're one of a kind, Christina Dimadis, one of a kind."

Christina's face heated, but the heat was swallowed by an internal vacuum when she remembered the gelato fiasco. "Actually, last week we ended up there and it didn't turn out so good."

"Christina."

Linda's tone lassoed around her gut and squeezed out the lingering dregs of negativity.

She tapped the rearview mirror. "See that?"

Linda glanced from the mirror to her with squinting eyes.

"That's the past. The backyard of doom is dust."

"We're going to go to the Spiegeltent, in case she's gone back there. And it's not far from where we met. You have no idea how many times we both ended up at that spot on the Yarra without planning," said PETER.

He swung into St Kilda Boulevard. The band truck followed, but Theo mistakenly turned into the horse and buggy lane. They had to crawl for a while before they could get back into the car lane.

"Bugger, we've lost the band."

Keith looked back through the rear window.

Despite his urgency, he didn't drive recklessly. He was definitely faster than Keith, but so were the horse and buggies sometimes. Maybe it would wear off after a while, but he liked the ambience of the horse lane alongside the cycling and car lanes. He found comfort in going with the natural traffic flow.

"We have to talk about your mother," Keith said.

That bumped him out of his cruisy internal lane. This moment was coming at some stage. He wanted to do it properly but this wasn't the time. "Really Keith, now? I'm kind of focused on my own stuff."

"After you find Christina, I might not see you for weeks, maybe months."

He gave his mid-death crisis mate a smile, appreciating the gag and his positivity. "Look, I'm OK with you and Mom. In fact I'm delighted for both of you. Please don't ask me for permission to date her. Just get on with it."

Keith let go of the holding bar above the door and launched the biggest smile he'd seen on his mentor's face. He couldn't stop how Keith felt about his mom. Besides, Keith was the nicest guy his mom had ever looked at twice.

"You have taught me more than you realize, Peter. Your bravery in love and romance is... well, it just *is*. With most people, it simply *isn't*."

"You on the red wine again?"

Keith laughed. When he settled, he shifted in his seat towards Peter. "Just one question."

He gave a hesitant nod, but kept eyes on the road.

"How do you know when to go for first base?"

He glared at Keith with anger and astonishment that not only would Keith ask a question like that, but ask him then.

Keith burst out laughing and slapped him hard on the thigh. "I was kidding. Chill." Keith emphasized "chill" like it was the first time he'd used the word. It probably was.

He couldn't hold back a grin and took a little pity on virginal Keith. This obviously wasn't easy for him. "You can never plan the special little moments Keith. Anticipation and surprise are part of the magic. Just trust your instincts, you'll be a natural."

Keith took this in, nodding gratefully. "I feel like me when I'm with her."

Something inside Peter's creative soul jolted. "What?"

"Sorry. No more talk about your mom."

"No, no. It's OK. What did you just say about her? Just then."

"Your face is so intense, I can't tell if you're angry or excited."

He forced a smile. "No anger, just give me the words, the exact words."

Keith closed his eyes for a few seconds. "I feel like me when I'm with her."

He hummed the chorus melody of *When I'm With You*. "Perfect!" He veered to the side of the lane and slammed the brakes, stopping next to the grassy strip.

A few cars tooted as they swung around Keith's car, narrowly avoiding a collision. Keith hit the hazard lights button.

Peter kissed Keith on the cheek. "I love you." He pulled out the pen from his pocket and scribbled on his hand.

CHRISTINA glided her Mustang down St Kilda Boulevard.

"If there's one thing I'm sure of deep in my soul, it's that you and Peter are soulmates," said Linda.

"Since when did you become such an expert on soulmates?" said Christina.

"Since I found mine."

She whipped her neck around. "Really? When? Who?"

Crash!

Christina's car had veered to the side and smashed into the back of a stationary car. Not wearing seatbelts, she and Linda flew through the air. Christina caught a glimpse of the blue sports car they hit which bounced forward from the impact.

She landed face down on the bonnet of the blue car just as it rolled to a stop. Linda landed next to her, their faces squashed against the windscreen. Linda was opposite a hunched Keith, who had slipped down his seat, while she faced Peter, holding a pen.

Destiny and fate. She never had a doubt.

Linda indicated with her eyes towards Keith. "Him."

She looked at a horrified Keith and smiled, then straight ahead at a grinning Peter.

Keith jumped out and fussed over Linda, helping her off the car. "Are you OK? So lucky you can't feel anything."

Linda gripped Keith with her eyes. "Oh, I feel plenty."

Peter jumped out and joined Christina as she dusted herself off.

"Interesting place to park," she said.

"This is amazing, Chris. We both died from car accidents and now we find each other with a crash. It's another sign."

"Yeah, a sign that we should stay off the roads."

Peter pointed to the mangled front of her Mustang. "That's another trip the old girl didn't finish."

"Maybe it did."

"You were looking for me?" said Peter.

She nodded then her eyes tightened. "Weren't you looking for me?"

"All my life... and death."

A dramatic horn lick pierced the moment.

They both turned to see a tray truck had pulled up on the inside lane near them, The Nat Empire horn section already standing and playing.

"I've got a surprise for you. Don't go away," said Peter, taking off. As if she was going to run away now!

Her lips vibrated from the magic his kisses always launched. She placed the back of her hand across her mouth to settle them, warmth gushing through her.

Peter jogged to the truck. He took a piece of paper from Natalie and scribbled something. Nat studied it as the band set up on the back of the truck then gave Peter a thumbs-up.

The crowd building around them had stopped traffic across all of St Kilda Boulevard. Keith and Linda stood at the front of the inner circle. She'd never seen Linda glowing so brightly. She wondered how much of it was happiness for her and Peter and how much was for what lay ahead in Linda's own romance with Keith. She winked at Linda.

Linda fanned her face with her hand while she looked towards Keith.

Christina laughed.

Poor Keith. Despite his new clothes and hair, he looked like a young school kid waiting to see the principal, shifting balance from one foot to the other, arms straight. Lucky Keith, actually. Linda would lead him through the sweetest romance education he could ever dream.

"Hey, princess."

She whirled around to Peter.

How can someone look so hot in just a white t-shirt and jeans? And those R.M. Williams boots, of course. The ones I bought him. How many times has he resoled those?

His wavy brown hair looked good, still teasing his collar, but not as straggly as his crazy rock days. And chocolate eyes that melted in her heart.

The Nat Empire horns kicked off again with a cruisy melody.

"You have an entourage now?" She pointed at the band.

He shook his head and took her hands. Her eyes were drawn to Peter's ring-less finger. "You saw Jane?"

Peter nodded. "She's good. We're all going to be OK."

She had no doubt, fully in the moment, enjoying every little second of the build up to whatever he was about to say or do. However it was going to play out, it was going to play out with Peter and that's all that mattered.

There was an added dimension of anticipation because it wasn't a marriage proposal. There weren't any romantic rituals to tick off. It could be romantically creative, or sweet and simple. Knowing Peter, she wasn't expecting sweet and simple. Just one look at the band confirmed that.

Peter placed her left hand on his heart. Rhythm and heat pulsed through her skin.

"When I'm with you, I'm with me," he said.

"Seven," she said.

"Seven?"

She pointed to her Mustang. "Seven times we had to push this baby home, or to a garage and you never complained. Not once. All you did was make me laugh."

"Now you remember?"

The last time Peter had asked, she was consciously pushing him away because his patience with her moody Mustang was one of the sweet symbols of his unconditional acceptance of her, one of the signs long ago that they were soulmates. She didn't see the full meaning of her feelings towards him back then. He didn't just wave the flag of love in her heart; he helped weave it.

She took Peter's left hand and placed it on her heart.

"When I'm with you, I'm with me."

PETER kissed Christina. He heard the crowd cheer like they were in the distance, his senses lost in Christina. Her lips with that unique formula the world's most gifted scientists could never create; sweet and familiar as yesterday, yet mysterious enough to spice up his entire soul every time he kissed her.

His body relaxed as her arms wrapped around him. His hands searched her back under her t-shirt. Her skin had launched a million goosebumps and he wanted to caress every single one. He kissed her again, with more fire this time. Her body melded into him.

The Nat Empire launched into Peter's new pop-dance song and he took Christina in his arms and danced her around the road. Others in the crowd joined in, dancing in couples, groups and solo. He saw his mom drag Keith forward into a bit of space. They danced old-school; Keith twirled Linda… no, his mom was leading, for sure.

He pulled Christina close when it came to the chorus. "When I'm with you, I'm with me," he sang into her ear.

The final three simple words, inspired by Keith.

"It's beautiful," she said, tears in her eyes.

Christina's body flowed with the infectious beat. Dancing wasn't his thing but he never felt clumsy with her.

JANE and Laura ran across the park hand in hand and worked their way through the crowd. Word got out quickly when there was a sniff of a celebration Up Here. Plus, Harpo House was just over the park hill. They stopped by the mass of people near the band truck. Laura banged away on her tambourine — which had become an extended appendage since she opened the gift bag — with an interesting riff.

The singer moved to the edge of the stage and gestured for Laura to join her. Jane lifted Laura onto the stage. Laura slotted into the rhythm and joined in with her dance moves, not missing a beat on the tambourine. The tall singer winked at Jane.

Jane's pride glowed sweeter and more velvety than anything she'd felt before. She searched the crowd and her glow didn't lose any wattage when she saw Peter and Christina dancing in the middle. It was good to see Christina so happy again. And Peter. She was relieved that she genuinely only felt happiness for them.

A bar and food truck had squeezed through the crowd and set up on the lawns adjacent to St Kilda Boulevard near Jane. Some of the crowd quickly lined up.

The food truck caught PETER'S eye then he saw Jane. He pointed Christina towards Jane and waved to her. Jane blew them a kiss with two hands, Christina and Peter blew a kiss right back.

Jane did a slinky shimmy. Christina laughed and sent the shimmy back with love.

"Is that Laura?" said Christina, pointing to the stage.

"Yes," said Peter.

"She's gorgeous." Christina pointed to Laura then swooned with her hands on her chest. Jane copied her, nodding.

"You're right, we're all going to be OK," Christina shouted to Peter. She shrieked when he picked her up and swung her in the air.

Christina's shriek was one of the comfort sounds in his life. If he could replicate it in a song, it would be downloaded by millions and on high-rotation on every radio show. He pointed her to the Safety Officers and huge flashing signs on the boulevard: *SOULMATE REUNION CELEBRATION — LONG DELAY EXPECTED.*

Christina pointed him the other way. Linda's head rested on Keith's chest as they slow danced; a quiet romantic center in the storm of the party.

He followed their lead and pulled Christina in close. Before he closed his eyes to infuse every essence of her, he was struck by colors of the sun setting behind three tall buildings opposite the park, creating two shafts of light that trickled across the bubbling party. Three buildings, two merging light streams.

Maybe he'd write a song about it for Chris. A ballad as soppy as a big wet sponge. Yeah, she'd like that.

Something about two glowing paths that were independent yet would always shine together and share their natural colors with the world around them.

The End

*Writers sweat blood to get stories out into the world
and reviews are our super-food.*

*Every time you leave a kind review, you're doing a
wonderful deed for all writers, all stories.*

Thanks, Jim.

FREE SHORT STORY exploring the fun romance of Linda
& Keith. Including scenes not in Up Here, like their first
"That was juicy" date.

www.JimShomos.com/linda-keith-love-story

In memory of...

My niece, Natalie, died aged 13 on 23/01/2009.
My "Bubba", Sofia, died aged 57 on 27/04/1973.

My Bubba's accident, as she walked home from a
Good Friday mass, triggered a lifelong reflection
on afterlife which led to the premise of *Up Here*.

Natalie's tragedy inspired the lines: "Death
is hard on the living" and, "We get to live,
so we owe it to them to make it count".
My new life philosophy.

'The Nat Empire' is a tribute to Natalie's
accomplished songwriting at just 13yo
(and a nod to my favorite Melbourne band,
The Cat Empire).

Acknowledgements

With pride or embarrassment, I've been working on this story since 1998, my craft scrambling in the distance behind the powerful premise, pushed on by irrational perseverance. Therefore, these acknowledgements could be as long as the book.

Up Here began as a screenplay with many generous contributions. Laura Sivis joined me as co-producer for five years. Not only was her editing valuable in those embryonic days, Laura provided the beautiful idea of: "What if a soul couldn't be physically held against its will?" Many years later Louise Schultze gifted the story with a simple spiritual *feelosophy* of replacing the word "god" with love.

Other people who contributed their screen wisdom on *Up Here*, and/or encouragement to keep writing it, include: Sue Milliken, Sue Murray, Ben Lewin, Sue Brooks, Megan Simpson Huberman, Sue Seeary, Dean Murphy, Kate Woods, Mark Lamprell, Nigel Cole, Rebecca/Simonne/Joel/Seph (Village Roadshow), Robert Watson (Beyond Intnl.), Simon Barnes (Park Entertainment UK), Sandi Pepe (Gersh Agency), Chris Noonan and Mark Pennell. Richard Stewart, Sonia Louise Cousins, Jennifer Ussi, Aleksi Vellis, Fabien Liron (Gaumont), Jamie Carmichael (Content Film), Jenny Day, Lynn Maree-Danzey, Jonathon Teplitzky, Melissa Beauford, Tom Burstall, Eric Fellner (Working Title UK), Karena Slaninka, Ros Walker,

Claire Stone, the Australian Writers' Guild 'Pathways' program, and Mark Lazarus.

A special mention for Nigel Odell, Mel Coombs and Ewan Burnett for your mentorship, friendship and grounding humor throughout my screen career.

Jenni Tosi and Sue Masters for the Film Victoria development funding in 2010 which led to working on the story with script gurus Stephen Cleary and Michael Hauge. Amelia King at Film Victoria, your faith and financial support of *"forget the rules"* helped sustain me in this crazy biz and lifted my craft and confidence to another level. Helen Zimmerman for your insights into Jane as a psychologist and other character insights. Santo Cilauro and Lex Marinos for telling me way back in 1998 to "buy this screenwriting book and write it yourself"; advice of two geniuses or lazy friends. John Petridis, whose patience and comedy defies the accountant stereotype, and my jewel of a lawyer Jenny Lalor.

I wrote the first draft of *Up Here* as a novel in 2013. The pros that have helped my prose and persistence: Graeme Simsion, Kim Swivel, Suzanne Kiraly, Carol Vorvain, Dave Sinclair, Fionna Roberts, Vanessa Radnidge, Sarah Mayberry, Luke Devenish, Rochelle Siemienowicz, Melanie Milburne, Jen Kloester, Frana Graco, Nicole Hayes, Lauren Harbour, Jess Fitzpatrick, Efthalia Pegios, Michelle Sommers, Valerie Parv and Alli Sinclair.

They say "It's the *journey*." I look at this amazing list of people passing through my career and I say *"They* were right."

Many friends and family humored me with reading various versions of *Up Here*: Val Wade, Karyn Dais, Beata Gombas, Felice Friguglietti, Nick Dellios, Ana Georgiou and my sister

Mary (mother of Natalie); plus the endless enthusiasm and feedback on many drafts from Mary Christian.

Keith Millar was the first person to teach me "less is more" in good writing *(except for debut book acknowledgements, Keith!).* Larry Holmes saw my path as an author before I did. My cousin, Chris, couldn't care less if I was a writer or cleaner, he'd take a bullet for me, and I for him. Terry Damos, Gary Shaw, Nick Bolton, Con Dais and Tim & Angela Newhouse for their friendship and belief. Three close friends made me laugh, often at myself, fueling another burst of creative energy when I needed it most: Ted Smith, Paul Petridis and Bruce Glen.

My dad, Tom, for his creative genes, irreverence and humor. My mum, Helen, for her strength, energy and stubbornness which are the foundation of my persistence and stamina. To the special women who have loved me and let me love them, who helped shape Christina and Jane and my ro-man-tic soul. Which leads me to my gem, Megumi; your love and support has provided the stability for me to continue this creative madventure without blinking.

Thank you Les Zig for introducing me to Busybird Publishing: Blaise who guided me through the publishing process with a stress-free confidence, Kev, for designing the cover in my head better than I imagined it, and their tenacious editor, Laura, who "had my back" and made the final collaboration on this story's journey a professional joy (and part relief).

Over 22 years Jim's stories have skipped across film, TV, web, songs and novels. An international pioneer in web series, he has collected nominations and awards in Cannes, Film Victoria and the Australian Writers' Guild.

"I'm a ro-man-tic, hooked on exploring contemporary relationships through fiction. Sprinkling love, laughter and sneaky tears."

Rumors of an insatiable passion for Haigh's Chocolates, Arsenal, Melbourne Victory cycling and blueberry muffins. Sometimes cycling for blueberry muffins.

Up Here began life as a screenplay and was shortlisted in Top-5 of the Australian Writers' Guild 'Romantic-comedy competition' alongside The Rosie Project.

Jim's next book, Kissing Scars is a romantic comedy inspired by a true story. Publishing in 2021, you can get VIP release news by subscribing to his newsletter at:

www.JimShomos.com